Angela hadn't meant to kiss Shane, hadn't meant to touch him, hadn't meant to feel this burst of attraction.

Intending to apologize for overstepping an unspoken boundary, she tilted her head back and looked up. All she saw was the blue of his eyes. In their reflection, her own desires were reflected.

Deliberately she glided her hand up his chest and around his neck. She pulled him close and kissed him for real. Her lips parted, and she drew his breath into her mouth.

He didn't move. His body was like granite, strong and steady. Even if she'd had a momentary lapse of judgment, he would resist.

She stammered, "I—I'm sorry."

"I'm not."

CASSIE MILES

HOOK, LINE AND SHOTGUN BRIDE

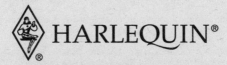

TORONTO • NEW YORK • LONDON
AMSTERDAM • PARIS • SYDNEY • HAMBURG
STOCKHOLM • ATHENS • TOKYO • MILAN • MADRID
PRAGUE • WARSAW • BUDAPEST • AUCKLAND

Recycling programs
for this product may
not exist in your area.

ISBN-13: 978-0-373-69496-9

HOOK, LINE AND SHOTGUN BRIDE

ABOUT THE AUTHOR

Though born in Chicago and raised in L.A., Cassie Miles has lived in Colorado long enough to be considered a semi-native. The first home she owned was a log cabin in the mountains overlooking Elk Creek, with a thirty-mile commute to her work at the *Denver Post*.

After raising two daughters and cooking tons of macaroni and cheese for her family, Cassie is trying to be more adventurous in her culinary efforts. Ceviche, anyone? She's discovered that almost anything tastes better with wine. When she's not plotting Harlequin Intrigue books, Cassie likes to hang out at the Denver Botanical Gardens near her high-rise home.

Books by Cassie Miles

**Rocky Mountain Safe House
†Safe House: Mesa Verde
*Christmas at the Carlisles'
††Special Delivery Babies

CAST OF CHARACTERS

Angela Hawthorne—As the young widow approaches her wedding day, she's haunted by memories of her first husband's death.

Shane Gibson—Though the deputy from Silver Plume, Colorado, has agreed to give Angela away on her wedding day, he suspects her groom of manipulating her.

Tom Hawthorne—Angela's late husband was Shane's best friend.

Benjy Hawthorne—Angela's three-year-old son was conceived *in vitro* after her husband's death.

Neil Revere—A world-renowned virologist, he seems like the perfect husband and father.

Yvonne Brighton—Angela's outspoken business partner in the Waffles breakfast restaurant has doubts about the wedding.

Josh LaMotta—The owner of Premier Executive Security Systems (PRESS) has hired Shane to work for him.

Jay Carlson—A medical student who looks to Neil as his mentor and is willing to do Neil's dirty work.

Edgar Prentice—The doctor who performed Angela's *in vitro* procedure knows the secrets of her birth and that of her son.

Eve Weathers-Jantzen—She and Angela have more in common than just being part of the same study.

Chapter One

A flat tire.

Tom Hawthorne slammed the door to his Toyota SUV, slammed it hard. Why the hell had he decided to take a shortcut instead of staying on the highway? It was the middle of the night, and he was stuck on this winding gravel road in a mountain valley. No other cars. Not a cabin in sight. Only the stars bore witness to his rage. "Son of a bitch."

Lately, things had been going wrong more often than right. He would have felt cursed if it wasn't for Angela.

The thought of her cooled his temper. He carried her image with him always, through the hell of the battlefield and the horror of working triage as a Marine Corps medic. Angela's sweet love made everything bearable.

As he opened the rear of the SUV, he took out his cell phone. Surprise, surprise, he actually got a signal.

She answered right away, as though she'd been waiting for his name to pop up on her caller ID. "Good evening, Mr. Hawthorne."

"Hello, Mrs. Hawthorne." Though they'd been married eight months, he still enjoyed claiming her as his wife. "I'm going to be later than I thought. I got a flat."

"Bummer. How was your night out with the boys?"

Boring as hell. "I'd rather be with you."

"But it's traditional for a Marine to blow off steam while he's home on leave."

One-handed, he hauled out the spare tire and the jack. If he'd still been a drinker, he might have had more fun on his night out with old buddies at a bar. The only alcohol Tom had consumed in the past year was a glass of champagne at their wedding. "The hour-and-a-half drive to the mountains was too long. And I lost twenty-seven bucks at pool. But you could make me feel a whole lot better, baby. What are you wearing?"

"Flannel pajamas." She laughed. "Are you fixing that tire or what?"

"Give me some incentive," he murmured. "Tell me about your sexy nightgown."

This was a game they'd played for years, and she was good at it. Her voice lowered to a purr. "I'm standing in front of the fireplace, and I'm warm all over. I have on a black, see-through nightie. It's short—so short that it doesn't even cover my bum if I bend over."

He closed his eyes, relishing a mental picture of Angela's slender waist and round butt. "Your hair?"

"Loose and tangled all the way down my back. Oh, and I have those highlights I've been wanting to get to perk up the brown."

"What kind of shoes?"

"High heels, of course. And silky black stockings. And a lacy garter belt."

"Baby, I can't wait to get home."

"Can't wait for you to be here." Her voice returned to a normal tone. "How long do you think it'll take?"

"It's after ten now. I'd say eleven-thirty." He set down the jack beside the flat.

"How's your buddy Max doing?" she asked. "Does he like being a daddy?"

"Looking at pictures of his baby was the best part of the night. I'm ready to start a family of our own." He looked up and saw headlights approaching. "Hey, there's somebody else on this godforsaken road."

"Maybe they can help you," she said.

"It's just a flat tire. I don't need help."

The other vehicle—a truck—jostled around a curve at an unsafe speed. He was an accident waiting to happen. Luckily, Tom had managed to pull onto the shoulder and had left his lights on. The other driver should be able to see him.

"When you get home," Angela said, "I'll make you some hot chocolate with whipped cream."

"Sounds nice." Damn, that truck was moving fast.

"I love you, honey."

The headlights blinded him. The truck was headed directly at him. What the hell?

The impact crushed him against the side of his SUV. His legs collapsed and he hit the gravel. The truck backed up. The engine revved. He was coming again. This was no accident.

Tom was a dead man. He knew it. He spoke his last words, "Love you, too."

ANGELA HAWTHORNE lay on her comforter, fully dressed, staring at the digital bedside clock as it clicked to that fateful time: 10:23.

A little over five years ago, her husband had been killed by a hit-and-run driver at exactly that moment. She'd heard the crash, heard his last words and then her phone went dead.

One-zero-two-three.

Her world stopped. Her breath caught in her throat. *Oh, Tom. I miss you so much.* She was poised at the edge of an abyss, wishing she could leap into ultimate forgetfulness and knowing that she never would lose her memories.

The moment passed.

A gust of wind splashed rain against the windowpanes. This was one of those summer electrical storms that started in the mountains and swept down to attack Denver with a fury. The distant thunder even sounded like artillery.

When she rose from the bed, she felt light-headed. She shook herself. Her eyes took a moment to focus as though she'd had too much to drink.

She slipped her feet into a pair of well-worn loafers and shuffled down the hall to her son's room. Benjamin Thomas Hawthorne, almost four years old, was her miracle baby.

After Tom's first tour of duty, he'd insisted that they create a stockpile of frozen embryos in case anything happened to him. She'd objected, mostly because she didn't want to acknowledge the possibility of her husband being wounded or, God forbid, killed. He'd soothed her fears and promised to come back to her, but his work as a medic meant he came into contact with a lot of disease. He hadn't wanted to take a chance on having his DNA damaged or becoming sterile.

Every single day, she was grateful for Tom's foresight. Less than a year after his death, she'd undergone the in vitro fertilization process. Nine months later, she gave birth to Tom's son.

As she opened the door to Benjy's room, the light from the hallway slanted across the foot of the big boy bed that had replaced his crib. He'd kicked off his covers and sprawled on his back on top of his dinosaur-patterned sheets. His honey-brown hair, a bit lighter than hers, curled around his ears.

His curtains—also dinosaurs—fluttered. His window was partially open, and the rain spattered across the sill.

She thought she'd closed all the windows when the rain started but she must have missed this one. As she pulled the window down and locked it, she noticed that the screen was loose. Something she'd have to repair in the morning.

After she tucked the comforter up to Benjy's chin, she kissed his forehead. He was an amazing kid, full of energy and incredibly bright. Everyone told her that she should start looking into preschools for gifted children.

Her fiancé was especially adamant on the subject of Benjy's education. She exhaled a sigh, wondering for the hundredth time if she was making a mistake by remarrying. No doubt, Dr. Neil Revere was a catch. At age thirty-six, he was ten years older than she was and well-established in his career as a virologist and professor at University Medical. He was wealthy, handsome, kindhearted and he loved Benjy. What more could she possibly want?

As she left Benjy's room and stepped into the hall, another bout of dizziness sapped her strength. She leaned against the wall. These nervous jitters had to stop. It was far too late for her to be having second thoughts about Neil. The wedding was Saturday. Three days from now.

When the phone rang, she jumped. Was she imagining this call in the night? Reliving the past?

She dashed into the front room and grabbed the phone, half expecting to hear Tom's voice. "Hello?"

"It's me, Shane. I wanted you to know that I'm running late."

Please don't tell me that you have a flat tire. "That's okay. I'm awake."

"No need for you to stay up. I'll get a motel room tonight and come over in the morning."

"You're staying here," she said firmly. Shane Gibson was Tom's cousin—the only family member who'd be attending her wedding. "I have the extra bedroom ready, and I made some of those macadamia nut cookies you like so much."

"You talked me into it," he said. "I won't be much longer. I can already see the lights of Denver."

When she set the phone on the coffee table, her heart was beating too fast. The erratic thump echoed inside her rib cage like a snare drum. She sank onto the sofa and concentrated on breathing slowly, in and out. Slowly, slowly. Her skin prickled with tension. A heat wave rose from her belly to her breasts to her throat to the top of her head. God, she was burning up. Sweating.

She'd felt this way before. Always at night. Always at the same time.

When she'd told Neil, he said her symptoms sounded like she was having a panic attack. He wanted her to see a psychiatrist, but she refused. She'd gone to a shrink after Tom's death and hated the process of talking and talking and never finding answers. As a mom and the half owner of a breakfast restaurant, she didn't have time to wallow in the past. Instead, she'd taken the mild sedative Neil prescribed for her. The pills usually worked. But not tonight.

Gradually, her pulse returned to normal. Leaning back against the sofa, she wiped the sheen of sweat from her forehead with the back of her hand. *I'm fine. I've got to be fine.* There were dozens of details she needed to handle before the wedding. Though it started as an intimate ceremony, the guest list had somehow expanded to nearly 150.

She'd be glad to have Shane here to help take care of Benjy. Shane and her husband had grown up together in a small town in Clear Creek County. Shane still lived in Silver Plume, where he was a deputy sheriff. Of all Tom's friends, Shane had been the most understanding. His was the shoulder she cried on.

And she had a secret agenda for Shane while he was in town. Eyes still closed, Angela smiled to herself. She planned to fix him up with the French woman who provided pastries for her restaurant. They were both tall with black hair and blue eyes. Obviously, made for each other.

Happy thoughts of matchmaking filled her mind, and she breathed more easily. *Everything's going to be just fine.* She dozed for a moment before a loud clap of thunder roused her. *No sleeping allowed.* She'd promised Shane that she'd be awake when he arrived.

Her legs were steady when she rose from the sofa, and she was pleased that her bout of nerves had passed. In the entry to the kitchen, her hand paused above the light switch. She saw a reflection in the window above the sink. A light? But that didn't make sense. That window faced the backyard. She squinted hard and focused on the dark beyond the glass panes.

She saw two lights, side by side. As she watched, they grew larger. Like the headlights on a truck. A ghostly truck. The lights bore down on her. Closer and closer. Coming right at her. They were going to crash through the window.

Reflexively, she threw up her hands.

When she looked again, the lights were gone.

A hallucination? No, it was too real. She knew what she'd seen. Without turning on the overhead light, she crept across the tile floor, leaned over the kitchen sink and peered into the yard. A flash of lightning illuminated the shrubs, the flowers and the peach tree. No headlights. No truck.

It must have been some kind of optical illusion—a trick of the light and rain.

She filled a plastic cup with water from the sink and took a sip.

A loud crash came from the hallway.

The cup fell from her hands and splashed water on the kitchen floor. The noise came from the direction of Benjy's bedroom. She remembered his open window with the loose screen. Someone could have climbed inside through that window.

She grabbed a butcher knife from the drawer by the sink, dashed down the hallway and flung open the door to her son's room. With no thought for her own safety, she charged inside. He wasn't in the bed. Frantic, she turned on the light. He was gone. *Oh, God, no.*

"Benjy?" Her voice quavered. "Where are you?"

Her heart thumped hard and heavy. She ran to his window. It was closed, exactly the way she'd left it.

The door to his closet was slightly ajar. Holding the knife in her right hand, she grasped the door handle with the left and pulled the door open.

With a huge grin, Benjy greeted her. "Mommy."

She placed the knife on his dresser and gathered him into her arms. She held him tightly against her breast—relieved that he was all right and terrified of the unknown danger that might still be in her house. *Something had made that crash.* She couldn't let down her guard, couldn't pretend that nothing had happened. "Why were you in the closet?"

"I don't know."

He didn't seem frightened. Wide awake and alert, but not scared. "Were you hiding?"

"I couldn't find my stegosaurus. I want him to sleep with me."

"Benjy, this is important. Was anyone in your room?"

"Mommy, what's wrong?"

She struggled to keep the tremor from her voice. "Everything's fine. We're going to be fine."

The doorbell rang. It had to be Shane. *Please let it be Shane.*

Benjy wriggled free from her grasp. She tried to grab him, but he dashed from his room and down the hall. Directly into danger? What if it wasn't Shane at the door?

She grabbed the knife and ran to the door behind her son. Loudly, she shouted, "Who's there?"

"It's Shane. I'm getting wet out here."

"Shane's here!" Benjy cried delightedly.

She flipped the lock and opened the door for the big, tall mountain man in his cowboy hat. She'd never been so glad to see anyone in her entire life.

Chapter Two

After years as a deputy sheriff, Shane was accustomed to dealing with crises. He read terror in Angela's eyes. Something had thrown her into a panic, and she wasn't a woman who scared easily.

He ruffled Benjy's hair and pulled Angela into a one-armed hug. "What's the problem?"

Trembling, she whispered, "I think someone broke into the house."

"Did you see him?"

"No."

"Do you think he's still here?"

Her voice cracked at the edge of a sob. "I don't know."

With a small child in the mix, this wasn't the time for a showdown with an intruder. He separated from Angela. *Was that a knife in her hand?* What the hell was she thinking? He scooped her son off the floor and said, "Let's go for a drive."

"You're wet," Benjy said.

"Rain will do that." He dug his cell from his jacket pocket and handed it to Angela. "Make the call to 911."

She stared at the phone as though it might grow fangs and bite her. "I don't want to contact the *C-O-P-S*. I might be imagining things. Could you just take a look around?"

He'd never been able to say no to Angela. From the first

time Tom introduced her as his fiancée, she'd been able to twist Shane around her little finger. Not that she asked for much or tried to manipulate him. Angela didn't have a devious bone in her body. She faced the world with a straightforward determination. A flame burned within her. Sometimes she was bright as a torch. Other times, like now, she was a flickering candle. He'd do anything to nurture her delicate fire.

"You said you might be imagining things," he said. "Why?"

"I heard a crash. Down the hall."

"Toward your bedroom?"

"Yes." Her lips were tight. Beneath the sweep of her long brown hair, her forehead pinched. She was desperate, stressed to the breaking point.

"I'll take care of this," he said.

He was pretty sure they weren't dealing with a drug-crazed psycho, mainly because they hadn't been attacked while standing here talking. But he intended to take her supposed imagining seriously. Until he knew better, he would assume there was an intruder.

From where Shane stood, he could see that the small living room and the L-shaped dining area were clear. The kitchen was straight ahead and the lights were on. If someone was hiding in the house, he was down the hall to the left.

"Here's what we're going to do," he said as lowered the boy to the floor. "Benjy, I want you and your mom to stand here, right by the door. If I yell, you run outside as fast as you can. Understand?"

"Yes." He held up his arms. "Can I hold your hat?"

"You can wear it."

When he placed his hat on the boy's head, Benjy giggled. "Look, Mommy. I'm a cowboy."

"You sure are." Protectively, she placed her hand on her son's thin shoulder.

"Why do we run outside?"

"It's a game," she said.

Suitcase in hand, Shane went toward the hallway. As soon as he was out of Benjy's sight, he unzipped his bag and took out his Sig Sauer. He almost hadn't brought his weapon. Firearms generally weren't needed at a wedding.

Moving fast, he entered the first bedroom, the guestroom that usually served as a home office for Angela. He looked into the closet and under the bed. Found nothing.

In the bathroom, he yanked aside the shower curtain. Nobody here.

As he approached Benjy's bedroom, he could hear Angela reassuring her son, telling him that Shane would be right back and everything was okay. He hoped she was right.

Except for the messed-up covers on the bed, Benjy's room was exceptionally neat. The closet was almost empty.

The last room to search was Angela's—the bedroom she'd once shared with his cousin. In a glance, Shane scanned the cream-colored walls and dark wood furniture. After he checked the small adjoining bathroom and the closet, he lowered his gun and returned to her room. A lilac scent perfumed the air; it was Angela's special fragrance. He never smelled lilacs without thinking of her.

Though he could tell that she'd been clearing out her things in preparation for the move to her new home, there were mementos scattered around the room. A tortoiseshell hairbrush set that belonged to her grandmother. A plate with Benjy's baby handprints. A handmade quilt Shane had bought for her at a firemen's bazaar in the mountains. Lots of photographs decorated the walls, including a formal wedding portrait of her and Tom. He wondered if she'd take that picture when she moved in with her new husband.

Finding no intruder, he closed the open window in her bedroom. He noticed that a framed watercolor of yellow roses had fallen from the wall, probably blown down by a gust through the window. The glass in the frame was cracked.

In the guestroom, he slipped his gun under the pillow, then returned to the front door, pushed the door closed and locked it. "No problem."

A nervous smile touched her full lips. "Thanks, Shane."

"I think I might have found what spooked you." He held up the eight-by-ten watercolor. "This picture fell off the wall."

"Ha! I knew I heard a crash."

When Benjy tilted his head to look up, Shane's hat fell to the floor. The boy scrambled to pick it up and returned it to his head. "Did you ride your horse?"

Shane crouched down to his level. "You know I'm not really a cowboy. I'm a deputy."

Benjy gave him a stubborn scowl. "A depitty cowboy."

"And you're a kid who needs to go back to bed. I'll see you tomorrow."

While Angela escorted her son back to his bedroom, Shane went into the kitchen. He'd visited this house often enough to know where everything was. Usually, the countertops were covered with fancy little appliances. Not tonight. Like the rest of the house, the kitchen sparkled. Except for a plastic cup on the floor and a water spill near the sink. Using paper towels, he mopped up.

All this cleanliness must be due to the Realtor's "For Sale" sign in the front yard. The house had to be kept spiffy for showings.

He found a plate of macadamia nut cookies on the small kitchen table and poured himself a glass of milk. This was a nice little ranch-style house in a good neighborhood. It ought to sell fast, and Shane told himself that he was glad to see Angela moving on with her life. When Tom and Angela bought this place a couple of months before their wedding, he'd helped them paint and move in the few sticks of furniture they'd owned. He remembered their high hopes for the future. After Tom finished his time in the military, he'd planned to go to med school and become a doctor.

He munched his way through three cookies while he thought of the good times and the bad. Angela was about to take another big step forward, and so was he.

She joined him. After getting Benjy back to sleep, she'd taken a moment to comb her wavy hair and pull it back in a ponytail. Though she was more composed than when she'd answered the door, he saw tension in the set of her jaw. Her cheeks were flushed. She'd lost weight.

"Thanks for checking out the house, looking for the bogeyman." She sat opposite him at the small table. "I guess I've got a bad case of prewedding jitters."

"I'm no expert," he said, "but most brides tend to get fussy about bouquets and cakes and seating arrangements. They don't go running around their house with a butcher knife."

"After I heard that crash, I went to Benjy's room. He wasn't in the bed. I was terrified."

"Where was he?"

"Hiding in the closet. I don't know why." She rested both elbows on the table and propped her chin on her fists. "I've been edgy, not sleeping well. You know how I can get. Not that I'm comparing a case of nerves to how I felt after Tom died."

He remembered. She'd been overcome with grief, and

he'd stayed with her nearly the whole time, except when he went back up to the mountains to follow up on the investigation into the hit-and-run accident that had killed his cousin. The detectives on the case had been competent, but they'd never apprehended the driver of the vehicle that ran him down.

He studied the woman sitting opposite him. A few days before getting married, she should have been excited and happy. "What's making you feel this way?"

"The wedding has gotten out of hand. I didn't think it would. Neil has a small family. Since both my parents are dead, I don't really have anybody."

"You've got me," he said. "And I'm honored to be walking you down the aisle."

"Tom would have wanted it that way. It's symbolic that you're giving me away."

He didn't like the way that sounded. He wanted to hold on to their friendship. "I'm not leaving your life. Or Benjy's. Like it or not, I'm always going to be hanging around."

"I like it."

She had the warmest smile. When she relaxed, he saw that candle flame inside her grow steady and strong. He reached across the table and took her hand. "Your wedding shouldn't be a burden."

"I've missed you." She gazed into his eyes. "It's been over a month since I've seen you."

"Anytime you need me, I'm just a phone call away." He looked into her eyes. The color of her irises had always fascinated him—a greenish-gray that seemed to change with her mood and the clothes she wore. Right now, they were more green, matching the cardigan she'd thrown over her white V-neck shirt. "Tell me how your quiet little ceremony turned into a monster."

"Everybody means well." She gave his hand a squeeze,

rose from the table and went to the sink to get a glass of water. "At first, I only wanted to invite my partner at the restaurant and the main chef. When the other employees heard, they wanted to come, and I couldn't say no."

Her south Denver restaurant—Waffles—was only open for breakfast and lunch. "Your staff isn't too large."

"Right, and I figured we'd have the reception at Waffles in the evening so catering wouldn't be a problem. Just a casual dinner. Then Neil's friends and coworkers wanted invitations. Doctors and nurses from the hospital. And professors from the university. Important people." She took a sip of her water. "Not that the woman who's working on a cure for malaria is more important than one of my busboys, but I want to put my best foot forward."

"I understand."

"Before I knew what was happening, I was arranging for tons of flowers and a DJ and imported champagne and a fancy cake." Her eyes flashed. "That reminds me. I hope you're not dating anybody special right now because I've got someone I want you to meet. She's French."

"Ooh-la-la." He hated being fixed up but didn't want to burst her bubble.

"On top of everything else," she said, "I'm selling the house, and it has to look great."

"Is that why you're still living here instead of at Neil's house? For showings?"

"For convenience," she said. "My house is five minutes away from the restaurant and from Benjy's babysitter. It's easier to stay here while I handle the wedding preparations. Neil lives on the outskirts of Boulder. It's a forty-five-minute drive, longer if I run into traffic."

It seemed to him that a couple in love would want to be together no matter how problematic. If he'd been getting married to Angela, he would have turned his life upside down to be with her.

"I'm here now," Shane said. "Tell me what you need, and you can consider it done."

She gave him a quick hug. "I'm glad you're here. When I heard that crash in the bedroom, I was imagining the worst."

"And it was nothing serious," he said. "The wind must have knocked the painting off the wall."

She looked puzzled. "What do you mean?"

"Your bedroom window was open."

Her eyes widened, and she gasped. "It was closed. I'm sure it was closed. I remember the rain splattering against the panes."

If that was true, someone had opened the window. She was right about the intruder. "Are you sure?"

"Oh, God, I don't know." Her hand rose to cover her mouth. "I think so. Is there a way to prove someone was inside?"

"I doubt anyone was inside. With all this rain, they would have left wet footprints, and I didn't see anything."

She shuddered. "What if they were standing outside and peeking in?"

He thought of his gun under the pillow in the extra bedroom. If somebody was sneaking around the house, he needed to secure his weapon. "Stay here."

He retrieved his gun and checked the window in the guestroom. It was locked. Moving fast, he surveyed the other windows and made sure they were all fastened.

When he returned to the kitchen, she was pacing. Her moment of calm had been replaced by renewed panic.

"Angela, listen to me."

"How could I be so careless? I know I should keep the windows locked, but I have them open during the day. When

I checked on Benjy earlier tonight, his window was open and the screen was loose. Somebody could have slipped inside. Into my son's room!"

"The window is locked now. I checked."

"I don't understand. Why would anyone want to rob me?"

He fastened his holster on his hip and put the gun away. Holding her by both shoulders, he stared into her eyes. "This isn't a typical break-in. Nothing was stolen."

"What are you saying?"

"This is personal." Somebody wanted to hurt her, to frighten her.

"How do you know?"

"I'm not a big-city cop, but I've seen my share of trouble-makers and stalkers."

"A stalker? Oh, damn. What am I going to do?"

"You and Benjy need to move out of this house as soon as possible. Tonight. Maybe you can stay at Neil's house."

"I can't. I don't want him to think I'm crazy. Or helpless."

"He's going to be your husband. If you can't share your fears with someone you love, who can you tell?"

"Not tonight." In spite of her raging fear, her voice was determined. "I won't wake Benjy again. I'm putting him through too many changes. A new house. A new daddy. A new babysitter. I can't tell him that mommy has a stalker. I don't want to scare him."

"I understand." And he figured he could handle just about any threat. "We'll stay here. I'll make sure we're safe."

"Thank you, Shane." She flung her arms around his neck and held on tight. Her slender body pressed against him, and he tried to ignore his natural response to having a beautiful woman in his arms. This was Angela, after all.

She'd been Tom's wife, then his widow. Now she was engaged to another man. Shane had no right to feel anything more than friendship.

But she was so warm. He closed his eyes for a moment as he embraced her. Quietly, he said, "I won't let anybody hurt you."

He heard the front door open. Still holding her, he drew his gun.

Dr. Neil Revere strode into the kitchen. "What the hell is going on?"

Chapter Three

Shane considered himself to be an honorable man. As such, he'd never seduce a woman who was about to get married to another man. Unfortunately, Neil didn't know him well enough to understand that finding Angela in his embrace was purely innocent, and there wasn't a real good way to explain what he thought he saw.

Angela left his arms and went toward her fiancé. She kissed his cheek. "I didn't expect to see you tonight."

"I told you I'd be stopping by after my meeting. You must have forgotten." He peeled off his wet trenchcoat and tossed it over one of the chairs by the kitchen table. As he tugged at his necktie to loosen the knot, he said, "You're forgetting a lot of things lately."

Though Shane didn't like the way Neil snapped at her, he cut the doctor some slack. Finding his bride-to-be in the arms of another man was damn awkward.

Ignoring her fiancé's rebuke, Angela forced a smile. "Neil, you remember Shane Gibson."

"Of course." He glared at Shane as though he were a virus that needed to be stamped out. "You'll be giving Angela away at the wedding."

Shane holstered his gun and shook hands. "I haven't had a chance to congratulate you. You're a lucky man to be marrying Angela."

Warily, the two men sized each other up. Physically, Shane had the edge. At six foot two, he was a couple of inches taller. He was probably five years younger and certainly in better shape, since being a deputy in a mountain community meant he sometimes had to go on rescue missions and sometimes had to break up bar fights.

Neil managed to smile without showing a bit of friendliness, which was okay with Shane. He didn't have to like this well-dressed doctor with the dark, serious eyes. The only thing that mattered was for Neil to be a good husband to Angela.

"Tell me, Shane. Is there a reason why you had your gun drawn?"

"Angela had an intruder. Somebody creeping around the house."

"My God." To his credit, Neil's hostility shifted to concern. He stroked Angela's cheek. "Are you all right? And Benjy? Is he okay?"

"Yes and yes," she said. "I didn't actually see the intruder, but the window in my bedroom was opened. And in Benjy's room, too."

"Are you sure you didn't just leave the windows open by mistake?" His voice was skeptical. "Absolutely sure?"

"What are you insinuating?" she asked. "I'm not making this up."

"It's okay, honey. I know you've been upset, having trouble sleeping." He seemed to be examining her as though she were a patient. What was wrong with this guy? He ought to be comforting her.

Neil continued, "Getting married can be very stressful, and I know change is difficult for you. If you're having panic attacks, there's nothing wrong with that. I'd like for you to get help with—"

"I'm fine." Angela's voice was strong. "If you don't

believe me about the intruder, talk to Shane. He's in law enforcement, and he believes me. When you came in, we were discussing what to do next."

"Is that so?" Neil wheeled around to face him. "It didn't look like you were talking."

Shane replied in a cool, professional tone. "In my opinion, there was an intruder, possibly preparing to enter. It's unlikely that the motive was robbery. Burglars don't break into a house when the owner is awake and walking around."

"What was he after?"

"Being apprehended wasn't the intruder's primary concern. He wanted to frighten Angela. He might be a stalker. Or somebody who has a personal grudge." He turned to Angela. "Have you received threats?"

She shook her head. "Not that I recall."

"Maybe from a disgruntled employee," he suggested. "Or someone associated with the restaurant. A supplier. Even an angry customer. Take your time. Think about it."

She sank into a chair beside the table. Her shoulders slumped. A moment ago, he'd been critical of Neil for treating her like a patient. Now, he was interrogating her like a victim.

As her friend, he knew what she needed. He'd seen Angela through the worst time in her life—after her husband was killed. She needed his support. Even though her fiancé was standing right there, Shane sat in the chair next to her and gave her a hug. "If you don't want to deal with this now, it's okay. We can wait until—"

"I want to get it over with," she said. "I'm thinking. But I can't come up with anybody who wants to hurt me. A couple of months ago, I fired a waitress, but she got another job."

Gently, he said, "Have you noticed anything unusual? Maybe had the feeling you were being watched?"

"I've been kind of spooked. Nervous, you know. Especially at night."

He considered the possibility of a peeper. Not usually a violent criminal. But this guy had opened windows. He seemed to be planning something more than just watching. "Earlier, we talked about moving you and Benjy to Neil's house."

"It's the obvious solution," Neil said. "I suggest that we get everything packed up and make that move right now."

She stood and confronted them both. "I don't want to frighten Benjy. We're staying here tonight, and that's final."

A muscle in Neil's jaw twitched, but he conceded. "All right, Angela. We'll do this your way. Have you at least called the police?"

"I don't want to," she said stubbornly. "There's nothing the police can do."

"You're being unreasonable."

Shane wouldn't have been so blunt, but he agreed with Neil on this point. "The police can dust for fingerprints, look for trace evidence and talk to your neighbors."

"I don't want any more investigating. Not now. Not ever again." Her eyes flashed with anger. "The police did plenty of investigating when Tom died. To what end? They still didn't find his killer. All their poking around was a waste of time. If you gentlemen will please excuse me, I'm going to bed."

She turned on her heel and left the room.

Shane's natural instinct was to follow her, to soothe her worries and offer comfort. But that wasn't his job. He looked toward Neil, expecting him to follow his fiancé and make sure she was all right.

Instead, Neil checked his wristwatch. "This is a waste of time. I have a lot going on with work, especially since I'll be gone for a couple of weeks on honeymoon. Coming here tonight was incredibly inconvenient." He glared at Shane. "And I didn't expect to find you."

Shane offered no excuses for his presence. Though he'd been planning to stay at a motel, he'd responded to the urgency in Angela's voice when she invited him.

"I suppose," Neil said, "that you'll be staying the night."

"I'm not going to leave her and Benjy unprotected."

"Fine. I'd stay myself but I'm in the midst of some very important meetings."

What could be more important than the safety of his bride and her son? Shane kept that opinion to himself.

"Tomorrow, we'll get them moved," Neil said. "I have plenty of room at my house. You're welcome to stay there until the wedding."

Considering what had happened tonight, it was generous for him to offer. "I appreciate your hospitality."

"It's no trouble. My housekeeper hired people to help out until after the wedding, and I have other houseguests. I believe you know one of them—Dr. Edgar Prentice from Aspen."

"We've met."

"He's a fertility specialist and an ob-gyn. Your cousin Tom sought my uncle out when he decided that he and Angela should go through the process of creating frozen embryos."

"I know."

"In a way, Uncle Edgar was Angela's midwife, even

though he didn't deliver Benjy. Ironic. Now, I'll be Benjy's father."

"Stepfather," Shane corrected. Nobody but Tom should be recognized as the father of Angela's child.

"I'll see to Angela now."

As he watched Neil stride toward Angela's bedroom, Shane wanted to stop him. Neil wasn't the right man for her. He was cold and arrogant and sure as hell didn't put Angela first. *None of my business.* Shane didn't have the right to tell her who to marry or what to do with her life.

He sat at the kitchen table, took the last macadamia nut cookie from the plate and bit into it.

When Angela lashed out against law enforcement, he hadn't been surprised. Shane had listened to hours of her complaints about how the Park County Sheriff's Department had failed to bring her husband's murderer to justice. She'd gotten to the point where she refused to even talk to them.

That had been his job.

The investigators had compiled quite a bit of evidence. The flat tire was caused by three nails that could have been picked up from any number of construction sites in the mountains. The indentations in Tom's SUV indicated that he'd been hit by a truck, and the crime scene investigators found bits of black paint. From the tire tracks, they could tell that after Tom was hit, the truck backed up and hit him again.

The police theory was that the driver of the truck was drunk or otherwise incapacitated. After he hit Tom, he backed up to see if he could help and accidentally ran into Tom a second time. The driver had gotten out of his car and had left a fingerprint in Tom's blood on the Toyota.

The print matched nothing in the database, and the cops had other factors working against them: It had taken over two hours to locate Tom's body. There were no witnesses. They'd never been able to locate the black truck.

The final conclusion from the Park County Sheriff's Department was vehicular homicide. The driver of the black truck was never found.

Shane understood Angela's pain and frustration, but he knew the investigators had done their best to solve the case. A hit-and-run accident was cold-blooded—the kind of case that would haunt the investigative team almost as much as it troubled Shane.

His instincts told him that Tom's death wasn't an accident. He was targeted, mowed down on purpose. Shane believed that Tom's death was premeditated murder.

THE NEXT MORNING, Angela felt like a new woman. Her usual schedule meant jumping out of bed at four in the morning and dashing like mad to have Waffles ready for business at six-thirty. Not this week. While planning the last details of the wedding, she had enough on her plate, so to speak. Though she might stop by the restaurant and help out, they weren't expecting her.

With no need to rush, she took a long, luxurious shower. When she meandered into kitchen after eight o'clock, Shane had already made coffee and fed Benjy. He greeted her with a grin and a joke about sleeping late. What an amazing friend! He made her laugh, always made her feel comfortable.

And he wasn't bad to look at in his jeans and cowboy boots. His black hair was in need of a trim before the wedding. Not that any of the women in attendance would notice. They'd be too busy swooning over his sky-blue eyes and rugged masculine features. It was hard to believe Shane was still single. There had been a couple of live-in girlfriends over the years, but he'd never once walked down the aisle.

After they dropped off Benjy at the babysitter, she slipped behind the steering wheel of her van and turned to Shane. "Before I stop by Waffles, I have to pop into the dress shop for a final fitting on the wedding gown. You don't mind, do you?"

"Bring on the ruffles and lace," he said. "I told you I'd do anything to help, and I meant it."

"Oh, good." The very idea of super-macho Shane in a dress shop amused her. "After the gown, we can go to the florist, then stop by the lingerie store."

He groaned. "As long as I don't have to have my toenails painted pink. Isn't the maid of honor supposed to do this stuff?"

"Yvonne's busy running Waffles. But don't worry. I'm sure I can come up with some manly, testosterone-driven tasks for you, too."

"Like moving you and Benjy to Neil's house?"

She hadn't planned on making that move until she and Neil got back from their two-week honeymoon in Baja. Even then, it would be difficult. His house was far from her work, her favorite market and everything she was familiar with. "It's so inconvenient."

"But safe," he said.

It hadn't escaped her notice that he was wearing his holster under a lightweight summer blazer. Shane definitely took her intruder seriously.

Not like Neil. She didn't like the way he'd reacted last night. In his opinion, she was having panic attacks, and he wasn't going to change his mind. Though she admired her fiancé for his decisiveness, she wished that he'd listen to her side of the story.

"After you're married," he said, "how are you planning

to run Waffles? You're at the south end of the metro area in Littleton and Neil's almost in Boulder."

"Neil wants me to quit."

"But you don't want to."

"I don't know." She'd given the issue so much thought that her head ached. "It's a bridge I'll cross when I come to it."

She turned off the main road into the four-block area known as Old South Clarkson Street. With several boutiques and restaurants, it was a pleasant, neighborhood place for specialty shopping. On weekends, traffic closed down in the morning for a farmers' market.

She drove past Waffles, pleased to see that the tables they set up on the sidewalk for summer were all filled. Around back in the alley, she pulled into her parking space.

"Why are we stopping here?" Shane asked. "I thought we were going to look at a dress."

"It's only four stores down."

She hopped out of the car and started down the alley. Though Shane's legs were a mile longer than hers, they walked at the same relaxed pace. When they were together, life seemed to take on a more natural tempo, almost as though he carried the easygoing mountain lifestyle with him.

"There's something I've been meaning to tell you," he said. "You're not the only one who's making changes."

He was always steady and predictable, someone she could count on. "What are you up to?"

"I'm moving to Denver."

"Leaving the mountains? You?"

"I'm turning thirty this year, and I looked around and saw that I was doing the same thing every day. Arresting the same drunks on the weekend. Driving the same roads. Living in the same house I was born in."

"Is this because your parents aren't in Silver Plume anymore?"

"Maybe so." He shrugged. "Mom and Dad moved to Phoenix two years ago. And my sister's in New York City. But this really isn't about family. It's about me."

"And you want to try something different."

"I'm taking a job with a Denver-based security firm. At first, I'll be doing bodyguard work, but there's training available. I want to get into computers. And I've been learning to fly a helicopter. Man, there is nothing like being up in the sky."

When she looked up at him, she saw a spark of excitement in his blue eyes. "I'm happy for you, Shane."

"Time goes fast. I didn't want to turn around and find myself turning into a sixty-year-old man who never left Silver Plume."

She opened the rear door to Linda's Dress Shoppe and went inside. There was nobody in the storeroom, which was typical. She called out, "Anybody home?"

Linda, the proprietor, stuck her head into the back room. "Hi, Angela. I'm busy out here. You go ahead and put on the gown. I'll be with you in a minute."

There was an informal sewing area in the corner with tables for cutting fabric, a couple of armless dress forms and a rack of clothes zipped into black garment bags with Linda's logo emblazoned on the front. A hot pink label stuck to one of the bags had Angela's name.

Since she hadn't wanted a fancy gown for her second marriage, she'd picked out a strapless dress with a bit of lace and a matching jacket to cover her shoulders when it got colder at night.

Shane stood beside a sewing table. "This is strange."

"What?"

"Right here, next to the scissors and spools, there's a kitchen knife."

When she took a closer look, anxiety shot through her. "It's a boning knife. And it's mine."

"How do you know?"

"The red dot on the handle." No one was allowed to touch her chef knives. When she wasn't using them, she kept them tucked away in a locker in the restaurant office.

She unzipped the garment bag, pushed the plastic aside and stared in shock. Her wedding gown had been slashed to ribbons.

Chapter Four

Unable to believe what she was seeing, Angela tugged the ragged edge of the ripped white fabric. The skirt had been sliced multiple times. Bits of lace hung like entrails around the bodice. The gown was ruined beyond repair.

Scared and confused, she turned away. On the table was the boning knife—her knife! Was it possible that she had done this? She couldn't remember. Had she suffered a blackout?

The thought terrified her. True, she hadn't been in her right mind lately. The lack of sleep and stress had taken their toll. Last night, she'd imagined headlights crashing through her kitchen window. But she hadn't gone completely insane. Not yet, anyway.

Shane touched her shoulder. In a low voice, he asked, "What do you want to do?"

For one thing, she didn't want Linda to see this disaster. The owner of the dress shop would have too many questions, and Angela didn't have answers. "Get me out of here."

"Done."

He tossed the knife into the garment bag with the dress and zipped it up just as Linda bustled into the back room with her long, silk scarf flowing behind her.

"Sorry to keep you waiting," she said. "I had a mixup

with the register. Thought I'd lost a hundred and fifty bucks. Then I remembered that I went to the bank last night."

Linda was a lovable scatterbrain. But not crazy. *Not like me.* She thought of Neil's diagnosis that she needed to see a psychologist. He might be right.

While Shane introduced himself, she gathered her wits, hoping to appear normal. Not that she needed to worry. When she was with Shane, other women hardly noticed her existence. Even without his hat, he was one hundred percent sexy cowboy.

He beamed a slow smile at Linda and said, "Angela is having second thoughts about the dress. She wants to take it home and decide if this is actually what she wants to wear."

"Brides are all the same." Linda grinned up at him. "Always fussing about the details. When I got married, I was as nervous as a squirrel on a highway, jumping from one median to another."

When Angela forced herself to speak, her voice seemed to be detached from her body. "Remember that white suit I tried on before?"

"Indeed, I do. To tell the truth, I liked you better in that outfit than in the gown. The suit seemed more…" Linda flipped the end of her scarf and chuckled. "More suitable."

"We'll take both of them with us," Shane said. "Then, Angela can make her decision later."

"Fine with me," Linda said. "But you still need alterations on the gown, Angela. You've been losing weight, and a strapless bodice needs to fit like a second skin."

While Shane went to the front of the store with Linda to make arrangements, Angela let down her guard. She sank onto a stool beside the cutting table and stared, unfocused. What was wrong with her? The inside of her head whirled like a blender. The shelves and boxes in the storeroom seemed to be closing in on her. She was suffocating.

She didn't remember taking the knife from the restaurant, and she sure as hell didn't recall attacking her dress. Was she sleepwalking? Had she done this in a blackout? *It didn't happen. Dammit, I'm not crazy.*

But if she hadn't done this, that meant someone else had. Everybody who worked in this area knew that Linda often neglected to lock the back door, and Angela's dress had been sitting here for several days, unguarded.

She stared at the garment bag. Who could have done this? Why did they want to sabotage her wedding?

SHANE ESCORTED HER through the alley. Though his hands were occupied with holding both dress bags, he was prepared to toss them aside if he saw an approaching threat. Last night, Angela had an intruder. This morning, her gown was attacked. Clearly, someone wanted to hurt her—or at the very least, terrorize her.

Adrenaline pumped through his veins, making him hypervigilant. Ironically, he realized that he was acting as her bodyguard. In a few weeks, that would be his regular job at PRESS—Premier Executive Security Systems. No longer a small-town deputy sheriff, he was already stepping into the world of big-city dangers.

When she clicked the lock to open her van, he placed the garment bags in the back and turned to her. "We can't ignore what happened."

"We can try." Avoiding eye contact, she opened the driver's-side door. "I still need to check with the florist and make sure the bouquets are—"

"The daisies will wait." He caught hold of her arm, stopping her before she shot off in a different direction. "We need to figure out who did this."

"How did you know about the daisies?"

"They're your favorite flower. White daisies." When she married Tom, it was winter and she settled for white roses. Now daisies were in season.

"I got my daisies," she said, "even though Neil wanted orchids."

That made sense. Orchids were hothouse flowers, expensive and delicate. Angela was a daisy person—cheerful and bright.

"You got me off the subject," he said. "We need to investigate, starting here at Waffles."

"Are you kidding? I'm not going to go marching into the restaurant and accuse my friends. These are people I work with, people I trust and care about."

"They're also the most likely suspects. They have access to your knives. They know—as you do—that it's easy to slip in and out of the dress shop through the back entrance."

She shook her head. "Nobody I know would be so mean."

"Let's think this through." He gently took the car keys from her hand. "When was the last time you used your knives?"

When she shook her head, her high ponytail bounced. Sunlight picked out strands of gold in her soft brown hair. "I don't remember."

"Think about it. Were you at Waffles yesterday?"

"I came in early to help with the breakfast rush, but I didn't unpack my knives. One of the waitresses was sick, and I filled in for her."

"And the day before?"

He could see her calming down as she considered the facts. "I put in almost a full day, and I was in the kitchen. So I must have used my knives. Believe me, I would have noticed if one was missing. I've had that set for seven years."

Seven years ago was before they met, before she'd married his cousin. He'd never really thought about that time in her life. Her youth. Her childhood. "How old were you?"

"Eighteen. I'd just graduated from the Cordon Bleu culinary school in London, and the knives were a present to myself—symbolic of my new career as a chef."

Shane wasn't a gourmet, but he'd heard of Cordon Bleu. "How come I didn't know you had such a fancy background? And how did you wind up in London?"

"When I was growing up, I spent a lot of time overseas. My dad was stationed in Germany."

He'd known that. "And your father passed away when you were just a kid."

"Not much older than Benjy," she said. "I barely remember him. My mom struggled for a couple of years before she remarried, and she worked in restaurants. That's where I got my love of flavor and texture." A tiny, nostalgic smile touched her mouth, and he was glad to see her calming down. "She died when I was a senior in high school. I had the choice of college or Cordon Bleu, and I wanted to cook."

"You were looking for something," he said.

"A taste." Her finger traced her lower lip. "You know what it's like when you bite into something really good? It's pure joy. I love seeing other people experience that sensation when they're eating something I created. Their eyes close. And they hum. Mmm."

He liked seeing her with a smile on her face, but he couldn't ignore the threats. "We're way off track."

"I know. And I'd rather not think about any of this. All I want is to get through the next couple of days."

"Whoever slashed your wedding gown is sending you a

message, and it's not a love note. I hate to say this, Angela, but you're in danger."

She turned away from him, stared across the alley at a six-foot-tall redwood fence. Her slender arms wrapped protectively around her midsection as though she were physically holding herself together. "What if it was me?"

He didn't understand what she was saying. "Explain."

"I might have imagined the intruder last night. There's really no proof that anyone was outside the house."

Earlier this morning, he'd inspected the ground outside the windows and found no footprints. The only possible bit of evidence was that the screen on Benjy's window was missing a couple of screws.

"What about the dress?" he said. "I'd call that proof."

"Not if I did it myself." Though the morning was warm, she shivered. "I've been an emotional basket case lately, and don't ask me why because I don't know."

"Something to do with getting married," he said.

When she looked at him, he saw a painful vulnerability in her eyes. Her mouth quivered. "I'm scared, Shane."

"It's okay." He pulled her close, offering his shoulder to cry on. "Talk to me."

"Being married to Tom was the best thing that ever happened to me, but it was a bumpy road. Right from the start."

Shane knew his cousin's flaws better than anyone. After his first tour of duty, Tom had a pretty serious case of post-traumatic stress disorder. And he was a recovering alcoholic. Before he and Angela got married, he quit drinking. She'd been good for him, helped him straighten out. "Tom wasn't perfect. Nobody is."

"This isn't about Tom. It's about me." Her body tensed. "Maybe I'm not cut out to be married."

"I don't believe that. You're a warm, loving woman. Look at what a great job you've done with Benjy."

Without thinking, he dipped his head and gave her a quick kiss on the forehead. Her hair smelled of lilacs. When she smiled up at him, the gray-green of her eyes seemed as deep as a mountain glen. Holding her felt so damn good; he didn't want to let her go. But Angela wasn't his woman. She was about to be married to another man.

"Thanks, Shane. You always know what to say."

He stepped away from her. "Let me do my job as an almost former deputy and investigate. I want to figure out who messed up your dress, and I'm starting here. At Waffles. Take me inside, and show me where you keep your knives."

Her eyes narrowed suspiciously. "Do you promise not to interrogate anybody?"

"Not unless they come at me with a loaded gun."

He strode to the rear door of the restaurant and pulled it open. Inside, the warmth of the kitchen flowed around him in a wave of breakfast aromas—bacon, coffee and freshly baked muffins. The back door opened into a hallway between the walk-in refrigeration unit and the office, which was their first stop. The office space had two small desks—one for Angela and one for Yvonne Brighton, her partner. Two tall, metal file cabinets stood beside two lockers.

Angela opened the locker nearest the door.

"You don't keep anything locked," he said.

"Sometimes I do. At the end of the day."

She removed a black cutlery bag from the lower shelf. When she opened it on the desk, he could see the empty slot where the boning knife should have fit with the rest of the set. Angela touched the space and looked up at him. "Now we know for sure. It's my knife."

It would have been simple for someone to slip inside

the office and steal her knife. The friendly atmosphere of Old South Clarkson Street made for lousy investigating. "I might be able to get fingerprints off the handle."

"Most people aren't that dumb," she said. "We keep a stock of throwaway gloves in the kitchen."

Though he nodded in agreement, he figured he could stop by the PRESS offices later if he wanted to check for fingerprints. They had a forensics department and computer access that rivaled that of the Denver PD.

Angela's partner popped into the office. Yvonne Brighton was a tall, big-boned woman who did a killer Julia Child impersonation. A lopsided navy-blue chef hat covered most of her curly brown hair. She gave them a toothy grin. "I thought I heard someone back here."

She charged at Shane and enveloped him in a giant bear hug which he happily reciprocated. He liked Yvonne. She was funny and smart—too smart to put anything over on. Before she stepped away from him, she patted his shoulder holster and said, "Expecting trouble?"

"Shane has a new job." Angela rushed to explain. "He's working for a bodyguard company."

His new employer was far more complex, but he didn't correct her. "I'm moving to Denver."

"Terrific!" Yvonne wiggled her eyebrows. "Or should I say *très magnifique!* Angela and I have somebody you really need to meet."

"The French woman." He gritted his teeth. What was it about a single man that turned women into matchmakers?

"Marie Devereaux. Very pretty. And an excellent baker. She's doing the wedding cake, which means it'll be beautiful and taste good, too. You'll like her."

"If you say so."

"I most certainly do."

Yvonne wasn't shy about giving orders. When it came to managing the restaurant, she and Angela complemented each other perfectly. Angela provided the empathetic voice of reason, and Yvonne made sure things got done.

She sat in the swivel chair behind her desk. To Angela, she said, "I'm glad you're here. I need a break. Could you take care of the kitchen for a couple of minutes while I chat with the mountain man?"

"No problem." Angela grabbed her knives and went toward the office door. "I feel guilty about not being here more often this week."

When she left the office, Shane positioned himself in the doorway so he could keep an eye on her. Despite the cozy atmosphere of Waffles, he hadn't forgotten the danger.

"We need to talk." When Yvonne pulled off her chef's hat and ruffled her hair, he noticed a few more strands of gray. He didn't know Yvonne's age, but she had two grown daughters. She exhaled a sigh. "I'm worried about Angela."

"I'm listening."

"She's been dragging in here like she's half-dead. Dark circles under her eyes. Hair hanging limp. I've seen her hands trembling. And she must have lost ten pounds in the last two weeks." Yvonne scowled. "It reminds me of how she fell apart after Tom's death."

"I remember." Though Angela and Yvonne weren't in business together five years ago, they'd been friends. "You and your husband helped her through that tragedy."

"And you. In spite of the grief you were carrying, you were one hundred percent there for our girl."

In the kitchen, he saw Angela step up to the grill. Her hands moved nimbly as she poured batter and flipped pancakes. She sprinkled powdered sugar on one order, dropped a dollop of sour cream topped with three blueberries on another. Graceful and fast, never missing a beat, her food preparation was a virtuoso performance.

Shane turned his attention toward Yvonne. Her concern was obvious and sincere, and she knew Angela better than almost anyone else. "Why do you think she's upset?"

"It's almost like she's haunted."

"Nervous about getting married again," he suggested.

"Oh, I don't think marriage bothers her."

"Then what?"

"It's Neil," she said. "He thinks running Waffles is beneath her. His wife should stay at home and tend to his needs. Can you see Angela doing that? Within a month, she'd be climbing the walls."

"If Neil gets his way and Angela quits, what happens to Waffles?"

"I'd sell the place," she said without hesitation. "We've had offers."

Yvonne's theory didn't tell him much about possible intruders or the person who slashed the wedding gown. Instead, it pointed back to Angela herself. Her fear of getting married—to Neil or anyone else—was eating at her, making it hard for her to sleep.

Still, he found it hard to believe that she'd destroyed her wedding dress in the throes of a blackout. Whether awake or asleep, Angela wasn't the type of person who committed outright vandalism.

He turned to Yvonne. "You seem pretty sure about Neil."

"I am." For emphasis, she slammed the flat of her hand on the desktop. "She shouldn't marry him, and I'll do just about anything to stop her."

Chapter Five

From his car seat in the back of the van, Benjy chanted in a singsong voice, "George Washington, John Adams, Thomas Jefferson."

Angela asked, "And who is president number thirteen?"

"Easy," Benjy said. "Millard Fillmore. And twenty-three is Benjy Harrison. He's the best. He's got my name."

Her son had an uncanny gift for memorization. He could repeat an entire book back to her after she read it aloud just once. He rattled off the multisyllable names of dinosaurs without a glitch. And he loved lists, like the presidents.

From the driver's seat, Shane said, "What number is Teddy Roosevelt?"

"You mean *Theodore* Roosevelt," Benjy said. "Twenty-six."

"*Theodore* used to visit Colorado a lot," Shane said. "The next time I take you up to the mountains, I'll show you a hunting lodge where he stayed."

"Mommy, I want to go to the mountains. Now."

"Soon," Angela promised. To Shane she said, "Turn left at the next stop sign."

Nervously, she checked her wristwatch. They were running late.

After Shane convinced her that it wasn't smart to stay

at her house, she'd packed up a few essentials and some of Benjy's toys. Neil's house was safer. Not that it was a fortress, but he had a top-notch security system.

When she'd called Neil and told him their plan, he sounded pleased, which didn't surprise her a bit. Neil liked to have things under control—his control.

They'd made arrangements to meet at his house at one o'clock sharp for lunch. It was past that time now. Angela fidgeted in the passenger seat, knowing that Neil's house-keeper, Wilma, would be annoyed. Her thin mouth would pull down in a disapproving frown, and her eyes would fill with judgment.

At the stop sign before they entered Neil's cul-de-sac, a black truck crossed in front of them. Thousands of similar vehicles cruised the streets of Denver, but every time she saw one, she was reminded of the hit-and-run driver who killed Tom. The black truck was a bad omen.

"Straight ahead." She pointed. "Pull into the drive-way."

Shane gave a low whistle. "Wow. That's a whole lot of house."

Three stories in English Tudor style, Neil's seven-bedroom house took up the end of a cul-de-sac that bordered on forested land. His perfectly manicured lawn stretched like a green carpet to the double-wide oak doors beneath the porch. Summer flowers and cultivated rosebushes, which were tended twice a week by gardeners, made brilliant splashes of crimson, yellow and purple.

Every time she beheld this magnificent house, Angela wondered how she'd handle the responsibility of caring for the property. Being mistress of the manor didn't come natu-rally to her. With the gardeners and the housekeeper and the people who came to clean, she felt as if she was moving into a hotel instead of a home that was truly her own.

As soon as they parked, Benjy threw off his seat belt and scrambled free from the car seat. "Open the door, Mommy."

To Shane, she said, "We can leave the suitcases here for now. We're already eight minutes late for lunch."

"Is that a problem?"

She didn't want to admit that she was worried about the housekeeper's opinion and trying her best to live up to everybody's expectations. "I like to be on time."

As soon as she opened the van door for Benjy, he jumped out. With his backpack tucked under his arm, he bounced along the sidewalk to the porch.

Neil opened the door and stood there, framed by his grand and beautiful home. In his white shirt with the open collar and his gray linen slacks, he looked elegant. Lean and healthy, he had a summer tan from playing golf and tennis. His sandy-blond hair curled above his forehead. His best features, as far as she was concerned, were his dark eyes. There was a fierceness in those eyes, an indication of passions that ran deeper than his sophisticated outer veneer.

When he lifted Benjy in his arms and gave the boy a hug, her tension eased a bit. She could see that Neil cared about her son. Marrying him wasn't a mistake.

As she and Shane approached the porch, Neil said, "I have a surprise. My dad just arrived from Virginia."

She stiffened her spine. Only once before had she met Roger Revere, retired general and former JAG lawyer. He'd made it very clear that she needed to shape up if she truly wanted to be a member of their family. He would certainly disapprove of her disheveled hair, the smear of cooking grease on her chinos and her well-worn sneakers.

"You boys go ahead to lunch," she said. "Start without me. I need to freshen up."

"Take your time," Neil said as he carried Benjy through the foyer to the dining room.

Shane hung back. He touched her arm. "Are you okay?"

Not okay. I'm a wreck. She felt like a big, fat mess—confused and borderline nuts. "I'll make it."

"Whatever you need, I'm here for you."

His offer of unconditional support touched her. Everybody else in her life made demands and passed judgment. Not Shane. He'd seen her at her worst, and he was still her friend.

Forcing a grin, she turned away from him. "Start without me. I'll be there in a jiffy."

She darted up the stairs to the second-floor master bedroom she would be sharing with Neil, probably from this day forward. The black-and-white décor felt sterile and cold. The only pictures on the walls were black-and-white photographs of landscapes—places she'd never been. In the adjoining bathroom, she closed the door and leaned against it.

The tension she'd been holding at bay coiled tightly around her, squeezing her lungs and making her heart beat too fast. No matter how fiercely she denied the threat, she felt danger all around. Either she was going insane or someone was after her. *I've got to calm down.*

She dug into her purse and took out the amber vial of the prescription sedatives Neil had given her. She was only supposed to take one at night before bed, but she needed to quell her rising fears. Even if she fell asleep this afternoon, that was better than running through the house screaming.

Popping off the cap, she tapped a light blue pill into her hand and swallowed it dry. Soon, she'd be more relaxed.

In the mirror over the sink, she confronted her reflection and groaned. Making herself presentable was going to take more than a fresh coat of lipstick. This would require a major repair job.

FOLLOWING NEIL, SHANE entered the spacious living room with a fireplace at the south end. When they were outside the house, he'd noticed two chimneys rising above the gables. As he'd said to Angela, this was a whole lot of house—big and classy with Persian rugs, heavy furniture and framed oil paintings. Two older gentlemen sat opposite each other in oxblood leather chairs.

One of them he recognized as Dr. Edgar Prentice. Prentice was the doctor Tom had used for the frozen embryo procedure, and Shane vaguely recalled some kind of recent scandal involving Prentice's fertility clinic in Aspen.

Slowly, Prentice unfolded himself from the chair. He moved with hesitation as though he suffered from arthritis. Even stooped, he was nearly as tall as Shane—taller if Shane counted the thatch of thick white hair.

"We've met before," he said.

"Tom Hawthorne was my cousin. I came to your office with him."

"And you've remained in contact with his wife for all these years. An admirable display of loyalty."

His comment made Shane's relationship with Angela sound like an obligation. Nothing could be further from the truth. "I'm privileged to call Angela my friend."

The old man's eyes lit up behind his glasses as he focused on Benjy. "This must be the young man I've heard so much about."

"I'm not a man," Benjy said. "I'm a kid."

"Of course. And what's in your backpack?"

"Stegosaurus, T-Rex, Triceratops. Want to see?"

The boy plopped down on the carpet. With much straining, Prentice bent lower, listening intently as Benjy unpacked his plastic dinosaurs and talked about the Mesozoic era.

Neil introduced him. "Shane Gibson, I'd like you to meet my father, Roger Revere."

In contrast to Prentice, the stocky, red-faced man sprang from his chair with impressive vigor. Shane braced himself for a power handshake; he wasn't surprised when Roger glared into his eyes and squeezed hard.

Though Shane wasn't a fan of macho games, he matched the older man's grip. It went without saying that Shane was stronger; he was probably thirty years younger than Neil's father. If he'd been feeling gracious, he would have let Roger win this little battle. But he sensed the importance of establishing dominance.

Smiling through gritted teeth, Roger continued to apply pressure. "I hear you're a sheriff in the mountains."

"I was," Shane drawled. "A deputy sheriff in Clear Creek County. But I'll be moving to Denver soon."

Neil arrowed a sharp glance at him. "Angela never mentioned anything about your move."

"Because I just told her this morning." With a flick of his wrist, Shane broke free from the prolonged handshake. "I'm taking a job with Premiere Executive Security Systems."

"Impressive," Neil said. "They're one of the best in town."

"I met the owner last year during a mountain rescue situation." The search for a missing client had been a harrowing few days, fortunately with a happy ending. "We have a lot in common."

Roger stuck out his square jaw. "I suppose that means you'll be seeing more of Angela."

"And Benjy," Shane said. "I sure hope so."

"Maybe you can convince her to cut down on her hours at the pancake house," Roger said gruffly. "The only person she needs to be cooking for is my son."

Though he didn't agree that Angela should quit her job and become a full-time wife unless that was what she wanted, Shane sidestepped the issue. "She works hard."

"Nothing wrong with dedication," Roger said, "as long as you've dedicated yourself to a worthy goal. As you know, my son has an acclaimed reputation as a virologist. He cures illness. He's saving the world, dammit. His wife should be something more than a cook."

Shane couldn't let Roger's idiotic statement go unchallenged. "She's a chef. Not a cook."

"What's the difference?"

Roger had stuffed his right hand into his jacket pocket, and Shane hoped that his muscular handshake had cracked a couple of bones. "It's hard to explain unless you've tasted her food. There's a damn good reason why her restaurant always has a line. She's an artist." He remembered a description Yvonne had once given. "A culinary artist."

"It's true," Prentice said as he straightened his posture. "Angela concocts recipes with the skill of a chemist. She trained at Cordon Bleu in London."

A tall woman with thinning black hair stepped into the room. Her long, skinny fingers twisted in a knot. "Gentlemen, it's time for lunch. Please come to the table before the soup gets cold."

Shane was hungry but didn't really want to sit down to a meal with these guys. He reconsidered his plan to stay in one of the guestrooms at Neil's house. Though he wanted to be close to Angela in case she needed protecting, he didn't like the Revere family—father or son.

"Before I sit down," Shane said, "I should see what's keeping Angela."

"You go ahead and relax," said Dr. Prentice. "I'll check on her."

As Prentice left the room and crossed the entryway to the staircase, Shane noticed that his arthritic shuffle changed into a confident stride. He was much stronger than he had appeared when he rose hesitantly from his chair.

Why had Prentice tried to create the impression of being a tired, elderly man? As a lawman, Shane knew that a man who lied about one thing will lie about another. He needed to check out Dr. Edgar Prentice and find out what else he was hiding.

SINCE SHE'D ALREADY moved many of her clothes to Neil's house, Angela had a lot of options. She'd chosen a cotton dress in conservative navy blue with white trim because it seemed least likely to provoke a response from Neil's father. As she finished brushing her hair, she heard a knock on the bedroom door.

Her first instinct was to lock the door until the little blue pill worked its magic and numbed her nerves, but she wasn't a coward. Slipping into a pair of navy flats, she marched to the door and opened it. "Dr. Prentice?"

"Angela, you look lovely—glowing like a new bride. I hope you don't mind if I take a few minutes alone with you."

He didn't wait for her answer. Instead, he entered the huge bedroom and closed the door behind himself. Though he didn't flip the lock, she felt trapped. "What did you want to talk about?"

In spite of his smile, his expression was serious, reminding her of the way a doctor looked before he delivered bad news. "Perhaps you should sit down," he said. "It's a medical issue."

Taking her arm, he guided her across the huge bedroom to a black chaise near the window. She really didn't know Prentice well at all. The process of creating the embryos took a couple of months, but she had only a half a dozen appointments at his office in Aspen. For the in vitro procedure, she had used a doctor in Denver.

She perched on the edge of the chaise. Her mind raced with dire possibilities. Was there something he'd discovered in her DNA? Some horrible genetic disease? Something that might affect her son? "This isn't about Benjy, is it?"

"Your son appears to be a remarkable child. Very bright. And healthy." He paced away from her. "It's best if I start at the beginning."

Suspiciously, she said, "All right."

"Twenty-six years ago, in the early days of in vitro fertilization, I was involved in a study on a military base in New Mexico. The Prentice-Jantzen study was designed to monitor children born in vitro throughout their lives."

She was the right age and born in New Mexico. "Was I one of those children?"

"Your parents were having difficulty conceiving. I was happy to help. I performed the IVF procedure."

She had never known. Her mother never told her. It was a decidedly odd coincidence. Both she and her mother had in vitro babies. Both times, Prentice was involved.

He continued, "Unfortunately for our study, your father received an overseas assignment, and I lost track of you. When you and Tom showed up in my offices and I ran your DNA, I identified you."

"Why didn't you say anything then?"

"It didn't seem necessary. You had your life in order, and it wasn't my place to complicate it."

She was beginning to have a creepy feeling about this conversation. "Why are you telling me this now?"

"Two reasons," he said. "The first is that you're getting married and should know the truth. And the second…" He paused. "Certain individuals have made allegations about the Prentice-Jantzen study. I want you to understand the situation from my perspective."

"Allegations?"

"I've always done what I thought was best for both the parents and the children. There are those who have accused me of withholding vital information."

Though he looked like an eccentric grandfather with his shock of white hair and thick glasses, he had the intensity of a much younger man. She shouldn't underestimate him. "What kind of vital information?"

"There were medical reasons why your parents couldn't conceive. There's no need for me to go into detail. The bottom line was that they would never have a child. The embryo I implanted in your mother was not her own. And not your father's, either."

It took a moment for Angela to fully comprehend. "The embryo," she said. "That was me. Right?"

"Correct."

"Are you saying that my parents weren't my biological mother and father?"

"Correct again. Using what was cutting-edge technology twenty-six years ago, I successfully created and implanted twenty-four embryos using the sperm and egg from highly intelligent, physically outstanding individuals."

She shook her head, trying to wrap her mind around what he had just told her. Her upbringing hadn't been ideal, but she had loved her mom and dad. They weren't her parents? "I can't believe it. This is impossible."

"It's merely science," he said.

"Why didn't Mom tell me?"

"She never knew."

Angela was shocked. Though Prentice had admitted that he'd withheld vital information, this was fraud. "How could you do this to them? To me?"

"I never set out to hurt anyone," he said. "When your parents signed on for the study, they desperately wanted a baby, You can understand that, can't you?"

"Yes."

Her desire to have a baby had been a visceral need. In the days following the IVF procedure, every waking moment centered on her ability to conceive. When she knew she was pregnant, her heart nearly exploded with joy. Had her mom felt the same way? Were they alike in spite of genetics?

"I gave your parents a precious gift," Prentice said. "I gave them you—a bright, beautiful, healthy infant. Do you think they would have loved you less because you didn't share DNA?"

"If they had known—"

"But they didn't. As far as they were concerned, you were their child."

And they had loved her and cared for her to the best of their ability. "I must be crazy because this is beginning to make sense to me."

"I expected as much. You're a practical woman."

"My biological parents," she said. "Who are they?"

"I can give you their DNA profiles, but not their names. The participants in the study—sperm and egg donors— were anonymous."

Prentice had offered a glimpse of a family she never

knew, and she wanted a wider view. "What about the other subjects in the study? I'd like to meet them."

"I advise against such a meeting. None of the others are your biological brothers or sisters. You, Angela, are the unique product of genetic engineering."

Was that good news? Or another reason for concern?

Chapter Six

—

The bedroom door swung open, and Benjy dashed across the snowy-white carpet with his little arms and legs churning. He jumped onto her lap. "It's time to eat, Mommy. Wilma said so."

Snuggling him close, she kissed his forehead. If it weren't for Prentice and for Tom's foresight, she never would have conceived her wonderful son. Life without Benjy would have been dark and grim. Unimaginable.

She stood, holding Benjy on her hip. He was getting too heavy to carry, but she was willing to strain her muscles to maintain the physical connection between them.

Looking beyond her son's angelic face, she caught Prentice's eye. "I have absolutely no problem with anything you've done, Doctor. I'm grateful."

With a kind smile, he reached toward her, linking himself with her and with Benjy. "So glad we had this little talk."

Neil had followed Benjy into the bedroom. He stepped up beside her. "That's a lovely dress, Angela."

"Thank you."

In spite of his compliment, she couldn't quite bring herself to meet Neil's gaze. Her talk with Prentice brought Tom to the forefront of her mind. Tom had been so insistent about the frozen embryos. She missed her darling husband who had died too young.

But she knew beyond a shadow of a doubt that Tom would want her to move on. He'd told her so. Because he was a soldier in harm's way, he'd insisted on discussing what would happen if he were killed in battle. Time and again, he'd said that he didn't want her to crawl into the grave beside him. If he died, he wished for her to honor his memory by living her life to the fullest. That wish was one of the main reasons she'd decided to have Benjy.

Moving on, dammit. She would be married, again. She would open a new chapter in her life. As they left the bedroom, she looked up at her husband-to-be. Even though she didn't always feel a zing when he touched her, Neil was a good man, dedicated to curing disease. "Dr. Prentice has been telling me some very interesting things."

"I know all about it," he said. "As a doctor and a scientist, I'm intrigued by your unusual conception."

"You knew?"

"You're a very special woman, Angela."

Genetically engineered, whatever that means.

At the top of the staircase, she paused. When she looked down, the angle of descent appeared to be as steep as a precipice. Her feet rooted to the landing. Though the sedative had surely taken effect, a wave of heat washed through her.

"Are you all right?" Neil asked.

She wanted to tell him but sensed that this was the wrong time to show signs of weakness. His father and his housekeeper would look upon her with scorn. Neil shouldn't have to make excuses for her; he should be proud of her.

Carefully, she lowered Benjy to the floor. "I don't think I'm strong enough to carry this big boy."

"It's okay, Mommy. I can go down all by myself."

While Benjy and Prentice went down the staircase, she clamped her hand onto the banister and took the first step. If she didn't look down, this wasn't so bad. Fighting vertigo, she took the next step.

When Neil touched her shoulder, it felt as if he was shoving her down the stairs. "You go on ahead," he said. "There's something I need in the bedroom."

Before she could object, he deserted her. She stood alone on the second stair from the top. It felt as if she was onboard a ship in the midst of a storm, and the deck was rolling wildly. It was all she could do not to grab onto the banister with both hands and weep.

Benjy had already reached the bottom. "See? I made it."

"That's good, honey."

At the bottom of the staircase, Shane appeared. Without hesitation, he climbed the stairs and took her hand. "You look good."

Her fingers latched on to his hand. *Please don't let go.*

He tucked her arm into his. "Here's a chance for us to practice for the wedding ceremony when I give you away."

Humming the "Here Comes the Bride" tune, he anchored her as she descended. His support reassured her. Without asking, he'd seen her distress and come to her rescue. He was the best friend she'd ever had.

At the dining-room table, she was seated between Neil, who sat at the head, and his father, Roger. Directly across from her was Shane. Beside him, Benjy and Dr. Prentice carried on a conversation about presidents and dinosaurs.

While she sipped the bland cream of tomato soup that Wilma had prepared, Angela had the sense that she was outside her body, floating over the polished oak table and looking down. She saw hostility between Shane and Roger as a streak of fiery red. In contrast, Prentice and Benjy had a mellow glow; they seemed to be bonding. Neil—the conductor of this weird color symphony—skillfully blended conversations and comments.

The meal progressed through salad and a particularly heavy casserole with predominant flavors of cheese and salt. If Wilma had been the least bit open, Angela could have improved her cooking skills a hundred fold. But that wasn't going to happen. The housekeeper had her own way, and she wasn't going to change. The running of the kitchen would have to be decided after the wedding.

After the store-bought cherry pie dessert, Neil turned to her and asked, "What else needs to be done for the wedding?"

"I have a list," Angela said. "At this point, it's just a matter of double-checking the details."

Neil touched her hand and smiled. "I suppose you have your gown all fitted."

Her heart sank as she remembered the tattered white fabric. "It's taken care of."

"And the reception?"

"Since we changed the venue for the reception dinner to the country club, there's no need to worry about the food. I know the chef, and she's good."

"Mommy is a chef," Benjy announced.

"And a very good one," Shane was quick to add.

Neil lifted her hand to his lips and lightly kissed her knuckles. "Is there anything I can do to help? You've been so busy, and I think the stress is wearing you down."

"That's true," Wilma said as she cleared plates. "She's losing weight."

"I'm fine," Angela said. And she meant it. The colors had receded. The vertigo had passed. Actually, she felt pretty good. "It's all under control."

"Glad to hear it." Roger pushed back from the table. "This might be a good time to deal with the business aspect of the marriage."

What was he talking about? "Business?"

"Pre-nup," he said with a scowl.

She and Neil had already discussed the need for a pre-nuptial agreement. They would both keep the assets they brought into the marriage. That part was simple. After that, the finances got complicated, and she'd left the details to her accountant and Neil's attorney, who also handled his finances.

While Prentice and Benjy went outside to play, Neil and his father escorted her toward the den which served as a home office for Neil. The floor-to-ceiling bookshelves held row upon row of medical and virology texts, including a book that Neil had coauthored and was being used in his classes. Afternoon light slanted through multipaned windows and shone on Neil's antique mahogany desk. The den always intimidated her, reminding her of how very little she knew about Neil's area of expertise.

She was glad that Shane had ambled along beside her—not insisting that he be a part of this proceeding but there to support her just the same.

Roger stood at the door. "This is a private matter, Shane."

Instead of leaving, Shane lowered himself onto the long sofa behind the coffee table. He rested his ankle on his knee, and leaned back. "I won't be a bother. Don't mind me."

"I most certainly do mind." Roger's jaw tensed. His dislike for Shane was obvious. And unreasonable, in her opinion. Neil's father was as slimy as a toad. He sputtered, "My son's finances are none of your concern."

"I want him here." Angela surprised herself by speaking

up. "Shane is one of my dearest friends. I have no secrets from him."

"It's all right, Dad." Neil stepped behind his desk and opened the top drawer. "This should only take a minute."

Grumbling, Roger seated himself on a chair near the window. His crossed leg mimicked Shane's pose.

Neil centered a stack of legal-size documents on the desk and turned them toward her. "The attorney marked all the places we need to sign and initial. Then dad will witness, and we're done."

She picked up the closely typed sheets. "There must be thirty pages here."

"More or less." He handed her a pen. "Some pages are nothing more than listings of property. The attorney thought it was wise to make everything crystal-clear. To avoid misunderstandings."

When she sat in the armless chair on the opposite side of his impressive desk, she felt more like an applicant for a loan than a bride-to-be. As she looked down at the pre-nup, the legal language swam before her eyes in an array of "whereases" and "heretofores." She flipped through a couple of pages. "Can you give me a summary?"

"What's mine stays mine. What's yours stays yours. And there's a whole other category of what becomes ours after the wedding."

Though she didn't want to make a fuss, some of these details might be important. "I really should read this."

"By all means," Roger said. He bolted from his chair and hovered beside her. "If there's anything you don't understand, ask me."

"Angela," Neil said, "look at me."

His voice compelled her. She stared across the desk. This was the man she intended to marry and spend the rest of her life with. "I'm sorry to be so difficult."

Neil's dark gaze linked with hers. "You trust me, don't you?"

"Of course I do." Trust was the most important part of any relationship.

"Just sign the papers. Then we can spend the rest of the day relaxing. It's a sunny afternoon. Not too hot for August. We can sit in the backyard and watch Benjy play." His voice lowered to an intimate level. "Maybe go to bed early."

It had been weeks since they made love. "What about your colleagues in town? I thought you'd have to go back to the virology lab."

"You're more important. Our marriage is more important."

Somewhat reassured, she looked down at the pre-nup. Reading through these clauses was a daunting task, but she was a businesswoman, and she knew better than to put her signature on anything without knowing what it said. "I could have my attorney check it over."

"You could ask him," Neil said. "But there isn't much time. The wedding is the day after tomorrow."

Roger snatched the papers from the desktop. "I'd be happy to help you. We can go real slow, page by page, so you can understand every comma."

She reckoned that he was trying to be kind, but she despised the note of condescension in his voice. She wasn't a complete idiot, after all.

"Excuse me," Shane said as he left the sofa and approached the desk.

Angela compared the three men standing around her. Roger was a former general and JAG lawyer, certainly a powerful man. Neil's standing in the international medical community gave him an aura of gravitas. But Shane was a lawman, accustomed to taking charge of uncomfortable situations. Though his manner was easygoing, he easily dominated the other two.

"Seems to me," he said, "that Angela needs her own legal representative to review the documents."

Roger bristled. "Are you questioning my competence?"

"Not a bit. But you're Neil's dad, which puts you in his camp. She needs somebody who's on her side."

"Don't be an ass," Neil said. "There's nothing contentious in these papers."

"Fine," Shane said. "Then there shouldn't be a problem. I'll take Angela to see her attorney and—"

"I've had it with you." Neil came around his desk to confront Shane directly. "Last night, I found you with my fiancée in your arms. Now you're stirring up trouble over a simple signature. Who the hell do you think you are?"

"Angela's friend."

Those two simple words rang with truth. Shane cared for her. He'd stood by her.

"Friends come and go," Neil said. "In less than forty-eight hours, I'll be her husband."

"Maybe so," Shane drawled. "Right now, you're just a guy with a pen and a stack of unsigned documents."

Neil took a step closer to Shane. His fingers tightened into fists. The tendons on his throat stood out. "She doesn't need friends like you—an ignorant, low-born cowboy who doesn't have two nickels to rub together."

Angela surged to her feet. "That's enough, Neil."

"Oh, please. You're not taking his side, are you?"

"Shane is my friend," she said. "Nobody—not even you—talks to my friends like that."

"His behavior is intrusive and unwanted. This agreement is between you and me."

"Then why is *your* father here?" she demanded. "Why

did *your* attorney draw up these papers? Don't I have a say?"

"Of course." He gave her a hard, cold stare. His eyes were as black as a starless night. "You didn't have a problem with these arrangements before."

"I never thought the pre-nup would be so complicated."

"Dammit, look around you. The artwork in this house is worth more than you'll earn in a lifetime. Did you think I wouldn't protect my investments?"

"I have something to protect as well," she said.

"What?"

"My self-respect." She took the documents from Roger's hands. "My attorney will be advising me on whether or not to sign the pre-nup."

"Wait," Neil said harshly. "You're not leaving. You wouldn't dare."

The hell I wouldn't. "Watch me."

Chapter Seven

Shane was glad to see Neil's house in the rearview mirror. If he had his way, he'd never return to that oversize mansion with the two chimneys and the perfect lawn. But that choice wasn't his to make. Unless Angela said goodbye to Neil, Shane had to figure out how to face her fiancé without tearing his head off.

Kneeling on the passenger seat, she was turned around, tending to Benjy in the back. The kid was having a minor meltdown.

"Not tired," he shouted. "Wanna play."

The plan had been to leave Benjy at Neil's while Shane took Angela to her attorney's office. But her son had a different idea. As soon as his mom stepped into the backyard, he'd run toward her. "Home," he'd shouted. "I wanna go to my house. Wanna play with friends."

Prentice, who had been babysitting, had gestured helplessly and said, "I don't know what's got into him. We were playing catch, talking and laughing."

Shane knew. Benjy was a smart little guy, sensitive as all hell. The boy must have sensed that his mom was upset. And he reacted.

Right now, Angela was doing her best not to show emotion as she talked to her son. "Were you and Dr. Prentice playing?"

"He's old."

"Yes, he is. What kind of games did you play?"

"I wanna go to Lisa's house." Lisa was the four-year-old daughter of his babysitter. "Lisa. Lisa. Lisa."

Angela prepared a juice box with a straw for him. "Do you like Dr. Prentice?"

"Mommy," he whined, "didn't you hear me? He's very old."

"But nice. Right?"

Shane figured that she was trying to find out if Prentice had done something to set off this tantrum, and he was pretty sure that she wouldn't succeed. Getting a coherent answer from a grumpy three-year-old was like asking a trout to sing.

She handed Benjy his juice, turned around in her seat and buckled herself in. Her gaze focused straight ahead, through the windshield. Her nostrils flared. Breathing heavily, her breasts rose and fell.

She looked as if she was on the verge of her own tantrum, and he would have been glad to see her express her anger. She had every right to kick and scream. "Where are we headed?"

"I should call my attorney before we go to his office," she said. "Get on the highway and head south."

He didn't know his way around Denver too well, and her van lacked a GPS directional system, but he didn't mind driving aimlessly if it meant putting distance between her and Neil. The disrespectful way he treated her was just plain wrong. When Neil talked about the pre-nup, he made it sound as if he was an aristocrat who had to protect himself and all his possessions from a gold digger. What a crock!

Though Shane didn't know the details of Angela's finances, she owned her home and her restaurant was successful. She wasn't rich, but she was doing well. Not that dollars and cents mattered to her. She was less interested in accumulating wealth and more focused on bringing joy to the people around her.

She finished her phone call and groaned. "This is one of those days when everything goes wrong."

"Your attorney?"

"He's in court today and tomorrow. And his associates are a married couple who are on vacation until next week. One of the paralegals in his office could read the pre-nup, but if there's a need to negotiate, I feel like I should have somebody with legal weight on my side."

Or she could postpone the wedding. That was Shane's honest opinion, but he didn't want to add to her burden of stress by pointing out that Neil had ambushed her. "Why did Neil wait until the last minute to give you the pre-nup?"

"Well, it took a long time to inventory his various holdings. And he wanted his father's advice." She didn't sound convinced by those reasons. "This has turned into such a mess."

He glanced over his shoulder into the backseat. "On the plus side, Benjy's already asleep."

She reached back and took the juice box from her son's limp fingers. "He was tired. That's why he was so cranky."

"You seemed to think that Prentice got him riled up."

"Which is ridiculous," she said. "Dr. Prentice is a nice, grandfatherly person."

Shane wasn't so sure. "What's his relationship to Neil?"

"He's a close friend of the family." She rubbed at the parallel worry lines between her eyebrows. "Prentice told me something that it's going to take a while to understand. It's not necessarily a bad thing. But unexpected."

"Do you want to talk about it?"

"Absolutely. But not right now."

He reminded himself to check out Dr. Edgar Prentice's background and current problems. "I have a solution for your lawyer problem. Earlier today, I talked to my new boss at PRESS."

"PRESS?"

"Premier Executive Security Systems," he said. "The head of the company, Josh LaMotta, has a law degree. He's not currently practicing, but I'm guessing that he's a heavy-duty negotiator—a five-hundred-pound legal gorilla."

"Let's go see him."

He merged onto the highway. The PRESS offices were at the south end of town in the Tech Center near Centennial Airport, where they kept the company helicopter. Shane made a quick call on his hands-free cell phone to confirm that Josh was in.

After driving a few minutes in silence, he became aware that she was watching him. "Something on your mind?"

"You must get tired of always having to ride to my rescue."

"Much as I'd like to take credit for being a hero, it's not true. You're too strong and capable to be a damsel in distress. You do a fine job of taking care of yourself and Benjy."

"It feels like I'm falling apart. I had a physical not too long ago, and there's nothing wrong with me. But I've been having these dizzy spells."

"Is that what happened to you on the staircase?"

"Could you tell?"

Standing on the second step from the upstairs landing,

she'd been hanging on to the banister with a white-knuckle grip. "You looked like hell."

"Thanks a lot."

"Your eyeballs were rolling around in your head. Your knees were knocking. I thought you might just crumple up and fall over."

"It wasn't that bad," she said.

"Seriously, Angela, how often do you have these spells?"

"Usually at night when I can't sleep. I get hot, then cold. The room starts spinning around." She fidgeted in the passenger seat. "Here's the weird part. I'll look at the clock and see that it's ten twenty-three."

"The time when Tom died."

With only two days before she remarried, she must be thinking about him, remembering what it had been like the first time she walked down the aisle. She was taking a big step in her life; a certain amount of tension seemed natural.

He changed lanes. At three o'clock in the afternoon, it was close enough to rush hour that all four lanes on the highway were clogged.

She leaned forward to adjust the air-conditioning. "Neil gave me a prescription sedative to help me sleep. Sometimes, it works."

He was drugging her. "What kind of pill?"

"I don't know. It's robin's-egg blue."

"Did you take one this afternoon?"

She nodded. "It didn't help."

As a general rule, Shane was opposed to taking any kind of medication that wasn't strictly necessary. "Your dizzy spells might be a side effect."

"I already talked to Neil about that. He didn't think it was likely. These pills are supposed to calm me down, and my symptoms are the opposite of that. My pulse starts racing, and I get burning hot." A sigh puffed through her lips. "I'm just stressed out."

Still, he wanted to find out what was in those pills. PRESS had a forensics department, and they might be able to give him a quick answer. The problem would be to get his hands on the prescription without telling her that he was suspicious of Neil. Why would he drug her? It didn't make sense for him to give her something that made her agitated. It was to his benefit to have a smiling, agreeable bride.

She heaved another sigh. "I can't believe I blew up at Neil like that."

"He deserved it."

"You don't like him, do you?"

Not one bit. But he didn't want to make her life more difficult by criticizing her fiancé. "My only concern is that he's a good husband for you and a good stepfather for Benjy."

"He adores Benjy."

From what Shane had seen, that was true. Neil doted on the kid. "But you're not too happy about the way he treats you."

"Today wasn't a good example. He's usually calm and understanding. When we go out in public, he treats me like a princess. A couple of months ago, we went to a black-tie fundraiser for the hospital, and he rented an emerald and diamond necklace for me. I looked at the receipt, and that jewelry was worth more than my house. Neil thought I needed something to jazz up my plain black dress."

"You must have been real pretty."

"I guess." She gave a little laugh. "But it's not me. Not my style. It felt like I was playing dress-up at this big, sparkly, gala event. I would have been more comfortable in the kitchen with the caterers."

He'd always thought she was at her best when cooking. Whether stirring a fancy cream sauce on a burner or frying up freshly caught trout on a campfire in the mountains, she took on a glow of happiness. Humming to herself, she'd lift a tasting spoon to her lips and give a smile of pure pleasure. Emeralds and diamonds weren't needed to make her beautiful.

He wanted to believe that Neil appreciated her, that he knew what an amazing woman she was. "Have you done much cooking for Neil?"

"He's a big fan of my strawberry salad. He's conscientious about his weight, so he can't really appreciate French cuisine. Most of the recipes start with a pound of butter and heavy cream."

Shane's mouth began to water. "He doesn't know what he's missing."

"Neil is a man who knows what he likes. And I respect that. Also, he was telling the truth when he said that we discussed the pre-nup." Leaning over, she dug into her shoulder bag on the floor between her legs and took out the stack of documents that were held together by a metallic clip in the top left corner. "I might as well start looking through this stuff."

Traffic in their lane had slowed to a crawl, and he maneuvered to the left. At this rate, they wouldn't make it to PRESS for another half hour.

While she read, Angela hemmed and hawed. Her long hair fell forward in a shining brown curtain. She flipped from the first page to the next and the next without removing the clip.

Finally, he asked, "What does it say?"

"It's all about who owns what. There's a section about how Neil has no say whatsoever in Waffles."

"That should make Yvonne happy."

She thumbed through three pages. "There are a bunch of stipulations about if the marriage is annulled, if it ends in divorce after one year or five years or ten."

The whole idea of a pre-nup didn't make sense to him. Maybe he was old-fashioned, but he thought marriage should be about love and partnership and spending your life together. He supposed premarital agreements were prudent, like looking for the emergency exits when you got on a plane. Not that the escape route mattered if you were going down in flames.

She stopped rifling through the pages. Deliberately, she unfastened the metallic clip and removed two sheets from the center of the stack. "Dammit."

He looked toward her. "What's wrong?"

"More than I can say."

Her eyes narrowed to slits. He could tell that she was clenching her jaw. Though she didn't say another word, he could tell that she was furious.

ADOPTION PAPERS! Angela paced the length of the empty conference room beside Josh LaMotta's office. Neil had slipped an adoption agreement into the middle of their pre-nup. Did he really think that she was too stressed to notice?

Yes, they'd talked about the possibility. But they'd decided to wait before making a decision. The present and future custody of her child was of the utmost importance to her—not to be handled as a side issue in a pre-nup, as though her son were just another possession that needed to be declared and labeled.

The west-facing wall of the third-floor PRESS conference room was windows—all bulletproof glass—with a panoramic view of the Rockies. She stared at distant peaks as the sun dipped lower in the sky, wishing that the solar heat could burn away her anger.

At least, she was clearheaded. The moment she realized that she was looking at adoption papers, she'd decided that she wouldn't discuss custody in front of Benjy. Though he probably wouldn't understand, he'd surprised her on more than one occasion with his ability to comprehend. She didn't want him to think—not for one single moment—that his mommy wouldn't be with him for the rest of his life.

A half hour ago, when they arrived at PRESS, Shane introduced her to Josh LaMotta. Then he took Benjy to explore. Apparently, Premier Executive Security Systems was equipped with a great deal of computer equipment, a gym with a full basketball court and a forensics lab. Her only stipulation was that Shane avoid the shooting range in the basement. Benjy already showed far too much interest in guns.

She paced the length of the conference room again, pivoted and went back the other way. She hoped that she was overreacting, that the adoption papers had been included in the pre-nup by mistake. After she and Neil returned from their honeymoon and got settled into his house, they would discuss custody of Benjy. There were other legal documents that needed to be reviewed and revised as well—life insurance policies and wills.

She pulled out the chair at the end of the table and sat. In her will, custody of Benjy went to Shane, his godfather. Tom would have wanted Shane to raise his son. *And so do I.* She didn't want to change Benjy's last name; he was Tom's legacy.

But Neil would be raising her son, providing a home for him, going to his parent-teacher conferences, taking him to Little League games. Sooner or later, Benjy would start calling him "Daddy." A shiver ripped down her spine. Tom was his daddy, his only daddy.

When she heard the door to the conference room open, she bolted to her feet. Josh LaMotta had a serious expression on his face. She was afraid of what he might tell her.

Chapter Eight

While Benjy played with Josh in his office, Shane joined Angela in the conference room. Her jaw was tense. Her lips, tight. When she looked up at him, the color of her eyes betrayed her mood—dark gray and hard as steel. Nobody was going to push this lady around, and he was glad to see her determination. He wanted her to stand up to Neil.

On the long table, she'd made three stacks of documents. She rested her hand on the first pile. "These are conditions I can agree to without hesitation. The middle stack is 'maybe.' And the ones on the end are problematic."

"Tell me about the problems."

"Neil wants to adopt Benjy. These papers are the first step in that process."

On the surface, Neil's intention seemed perfectly natural. Her fiancé was a single man, and she was a mother with a child he loved. It seemed that Neil was doing the right thing, making sure that Benjy was taken care of. "I'm guessing that you've talked about custody before now."

"Well, yes. And we agreed to make those decisions later."

Her reluctance to assign custody said more about her state of mind than Neil's. She was willing to marry the man and have him raise Benjy, but she didn't want to think about giving up her child. Shane had a pretty good idea why she was disturbed. "This is about Tom."

"Benjy is his son. Benjamin Thomas Hawthorne. I don't want to change his name to Revere. He needs to know who his father was."

"I couldn't agree more." Shane wanted to preserve his memory as much as she did. "I won't let him forget, and neither will you. But Benjy might benefit from having a flesh-and-blood father."

"What do you mean?"

"You know what I'm talking about."

She turned her back and stalked away from him. At the far end of the conference table, she whipped around. "I know it's important for Benjy to have a positive male role model while he's growing up. And I know Tom would want his son to have a full life."

"You don't have to convince me."

"Here's something you need to understand." She came back toward him, one deliberate step at a time. "You saw me at the worst time in my life. You stood by me, and I'll never forget your support and your kindness. But I'm different now. I don't spend every waking moment thinking of Tom. Not anymore. I have Waffles. I have friends. My life is full, and Benjy is thriving."

Though she was looking straight at him, she sounded more like she was trying to convince herself. He said, "I'm proud of you. The way you've grown."

"I'll always be Tom's widow. But I'm about to become Neil's wife. I'm ready to turn that page."

And he wanted to be happy for her. Her life hadn't been easy; she'd lost both parents and a husband. But was Neil the right man?

He looked down on the three stacks of papers. "Did Josh have any advice?"

"He told me not to sign anything that made me uncomfortable."

"Hell, I could have told you that much."

"He's really glad that you're coming to work for him. He told me about how you met." She reached out, touched his shoulder and gave a light squeeze. "I'm not the only person who thinks you're a hero. Josh credits you with saving the lives of his three clients."

"Just doing my job." Mountain rescues could be a tricky business, and Shane had a lot of experience both in tracking and in pulling people out of dangerous spots.

"He says you're the best hire he's ever made."

"That remains to be seen." He had a lot to learn about personal security, especially when it came to the electronics. "Can we get back to Josh's legal advice?"

"The middle pile is about the possible dissolution of the marriage. Josh said it was one-sided."

"How so?"

"There were a lot of ways I could screw up and cause a divorce. But not so many for Neil."

From what he'd seen of her fiancé, that didn't surprise him. Neil wouldn't admit to any flaws. "What about the adoption papers?"

"I'm having a hard time dealing with the fact that Neil tried to sneak this past me. I've already made provisions for what happens to Benjy if I up and die."

"He comes to live with me." He reckoned that Neil hated the current setup. It might be one of the reasons he was so hell-bent on getting the adoption under way.

"You're his godfather." Her wistful smile contradicted the fire in her eyes, reminding him of her gentleness. "You'll always be in Benjy's life."

Not if Neil had anything to say about it. Shane was beginning to object to the adoption from his own standpoint. "Did Josh point out any legal problems?"

"There was a section defining what happens if either Neil or I become incapacitated."

"Incapacitated?"

"It's designed to cover dire circumstances. For example, if I go into a coma, Neil has full custody and makes decisions for Benjy."

"A coma? That's dire, all right." Legal documents seldom dealt with the good times. "But it makes sense. What bothered Josh?"

"The language was too broad. This clause says that Neil has immediate custody if I'm incapable in any way or manner—physically, mentally or emotionally—to care for my son."

"Does that mean Benjy could be taken away from you?"

"If I can't take proper care of him, yes." She glanced down at the papers. "I'm sure Neil is just trying to make sure my son is protected."

"From you?"

"Stop it, Shane. Don't make it sound worse than it is."

He couldn't ignore the threat. Being physically incapacitated fit her earlier example of prolonged hospitalization with a coma. But mentally? Emotionally? According to those vaguely defined terms, she could lose custody of her son if she had a nervous breakdown.

Her nighttime panic attacks took on darker implications. Had she imagined an intruder breaking into her house? Was she emotionally unbalanced enough to slash her own wedding dress? It wouldn't be hard for Neil to build a case against her, especially if she was living with him and taking medications he prescribed. He could make her look insane. He might already be laying the groundwork with his supposedly well-meaning suggestions that she should see a psychiatrist.

"The very same clause," she said, "applied to Neil. It's the same wording."

"But Neil hasn't been suffering from vertigo and panic."

"Usually, neither am I." Her lips pinched. "It's stress. After the wedding, I'll be fine."

"It wasn't stress that stole your knife and slashed your gown. You didn't imagine that. I was there. I saw the evidence. Someone carried out that act."

Her spine stiffened. "What are you suggesting?"

"Hell, I'll do more than suggest." He couldn't let her walk into this trap. "Neil is trying to make you look crazy."

"I can't believe that. He's a world-renowned virologist. There's no way he'd sneak through a back alley with my knife."

"He could hire someone to do it."

"But why?" Her voice trembled with anger. "To make me look insane and get custody of Benjy? Why would he want to do that?"

"I don't know his motive."

"Because there isn't one." Furious, she glared at him. "Whether you like him or not, Neil isn't a monster. He'd never do such things."

"Prove it," he said. "Give me one of those sedatives he prescribed for you and let me have the PRESS lab analyze it."

"Fine." She grabbed her shoulder bag from one of the chairs, dug inside and pulled out the vial. She tapped a pill into her hand and set it on the table. "Take it."

He slipped the light blue pill into his pocket. Tersely, he asked, "What do you want to do next?"

Moving stiffly but swiftly, she got right up in his face.

Her cheeks flamed. Her eyes shot daggers. Even her hair looked angry. "If you were anybody else, I'd tell you to go straight to hell. But we've been friends for a long time, and I know you think you're protecting me."

He *was* protecting her. Blinded by her imminent wedding, she couldn't see the danger coming at her like a freight train. "Correct."

"Let it go."

"Fine." Until he had proof, he'd step aside.

She tossed her head, and her long hair rippled. She flexed her slender shoulders, shaking off her anger. "Okay, then. All right. Can we pretend that we never had this conversation?"

"I doubt it." He wasn't letting go of his suspicions until he was proved wrong. "But we can call a truce."

"That'll have to be enough." She hoisted the strap of her purse onto her arm. "I need some time to cool down. I'd really like to go back to my house tonight if you think it won't be dangerous."

"I'll make it safe." *Safer than being with Neil.*

"As for the pre-nup," she said, "I don't know what to do. One thing is for sure. I hate the adoption and custody section."

He took those papers from the table and tore them in half. For emphasis, he tore the half into fourths.

Never before had he taken a strong position on what she ought to do with her life. His role had been to stand beside her and offer support. When she did well, he applauded. When she fell apart, he picked up the pieces. He never judged her.

As she looked at him, her eyes widened as though she were seeing him differently. "Well, I guess that decision is made."

"Damn right."

He didn't know why they were playing this game, but he'd make sure that Neil wouldn't win.

AT HER HOUSE, Angela stood on the front stoop while Shane checked the door to make sure the lock hadn't been tampered with. He bent down and focused the beam of a flashlight on the keyhole.

Benjy hovered close beside him. "What are you doing?"

"Making sure nobody messed with the door."

"It was locked," she said with some exasperation. Since the real estate agent hadn't scheduled a showing for today, she'd also fastened the dead bolt before they left. "And I have the key."

"Don't tell your mom, but you don't always need a key to open a lock."

"Really?" Benjy whispered back. "How does it work?"

"Magic," she said, hoping that Shane wouldn't insist on giving her son a lesson on how to pick locks. "Let's get inside."

Shane entered first and turned on the living-room light. He carried a large metal case imprinted with the PRESS logo. It contained the equipment for a top-of-the-line security system, which Josh LaMotta had been happy to provide free of charge with the stipulation that Shane do the installation as a training exercise. Though she was grateful to have the protection, she hated the necessity.

They'd already had dinner, but she went to the kitchen anyway. There was a lot on her mind, and cooking always helped her concentrate. As she washed her hands in the sink, she looked into her backyard, remembering her terror when she'd thought she saw approaching headlights through this window. Her panic was gone. With Shane in the house, she had no reason for fear.

He tromped into the kitchen with her son at his side and announced, "We're going to get started."

"Our house is going to be a fortress," Benjy said. He'd been excited and impressed with all the cool equipment he saw at PRESS. "With computers and valance cameras."

"Surveillance cameras," Shane corrected.

"Mommy, I want to be a bodyguard when I grow up."

"Not so fast," Shane said. "I thought you wanted to be president."

"I'll be both."

"Bedtime," she said sternly, "is in an hour."

Before they left the kitchen, Shane gave her a fond smile. Such a handsome man with his blue eyes and black hair, he truly was one of her best friends. It was impossible to stay mad at him, in spite of the terrible things he'd said about Neil.

She took a mixing bowl from the cabinet below the sink. Neil had left two apologetic messages on her cell phone, and she needed to call him back, but she wasn't sure exactly what she wanted to say. She was still angry about the way he'd dropped that pre-nup on her with his self-important father standing over her and looking down his nose.

She searched her cupboards. Since she'd been clearing things out, there wasn't much to choose from. But she could throw together a cinnamon and brown sugar coffee cake for tomorrow morning. As her hands busily sifted the flour and creamed the butter, her brain sorted out what she wanted to say to her fiancé.

There was no way she'd agree to the custody conditions of the pre-nup. On that point, she was firm. She'd refuse even if he insisted, even if he threatened to call off the wedding.

She groaned, thinking of the weeks of preparation that would go down the drain. She couldn't turn back now, she'd gone beyond the point of no return.

On the other hand, this marriage had turned her life upside down. She was selling this little house that she loved and moving far away from her business. Relocating Benjy presented another set of problems. Though she intended to keep him with the same babysitter when she came to work, she'd need backup nearer to Neil's house. He'd suggested a nanny, but she didn't want a full-time employee to take care of her son. Spending time with Benjy was the best part of her day. Why would she want to lose one minute of that precious time?

Neil really didn't understand what it was like to be a full-time parent. But he loved Benjy.

While she stirred the batter, she wondered. Did he love her? When she'd stormed out of his house this afternoon, he made very little effort to stop her. Not that it would have done any good. She wouldn't have listened. *How much do I love him?*

Her wooden spoon stilled. Planning the wedding had been so stressful that she'd forgotten the most important part. She and Neil hadn't been behaving like two people in love.

She spooned the batter into the greased pan and slid it into the oven. *Call him.* Back at the sink, she washed her hands again. From down the hall, she heard Benjy and Shane working on the security alarm project. Maybe she should go and watch them, make sure that Benjy was winding down for bedtime. *Call him.* She went to the fridge and looked inside. There were plenty of eggs and some wonderful baby Swiss cheese from the deli on Arapahoe. It might be handy to make a quiche. You could never go wrong with quiche.

Firmly she closed the refrigerator door, went to her purse and took out her cell phone. Neil would be her husband—the man she would share her life with.

She had to make this call.

Chapter Nine

After she'd gotten Benjy to bed, Angela opened a bottle of cabernet for her and Shane. Having a glass of wine at night was a simple ritual they'd started while she was struggling with the demands of being a new mother. While she was married to Tom, she'd never kept alcohol in the house, which was a huge sacrifice for a chef because wine was the perfect complement to so many foods. She didn't consider herself to be a wine connoisseur, but she had an excellent palate.

Sitting opposite each other at the kitchen table, they clinked glasses, and she offered a toast. *"A votre santé."* To your health.

"Cheers," he responded.

She took a sip of the full-bodied French wine, tasting a hint of mushroom and oak and enjoying the companionable moment. Spending time with Shane always seemed to put things into perspective.

"I called Neil and told him we'd be staying at my house tonight," she said. "He agreed to change the pre-nup. No problem. He'll take out the adoption section and the pages that pertained to cause for divorce."

"Leaving only the part about dividing up property."

"That's right." Neil's cooperation justified her trust in

him. On the phone, he'd been apologetic. "He's willing to bend over backward to make me happy."

"And get your signature." Though Shane restrained himself from scoffing, his gaze radiated pure cynicism. "I don't suppose he had an explanation for why he put in those clauses about being mentally or emotionally incapacitated."

"I didn't ask. I'm sure it was just some kind of lawyer language."

At least, that was what she told herself. She had to believe that her fiancé had no sinister ulterior motives. If Neil truly was trying to take Benjy away from her, she couldn't go through with the wedding. More than that, she had to run away from him—as far and as fast as she could.

Staring into the ruby wine, she said, "Tomorrow night is the rehearsal dinner. Neil asked if you'd be bringing a date and I told him you would."

"Great," he said with a grin. "I'll bring Josh."

"What?"

"It might be handy to have a negotiator on hand when you sign the pre-nup."

She hadn't thought that far ahead, but she wouldn't mind having backup when she faced Neil and his father. "That's okay with me, but what about Josh? He's already been incredibly helpful. I don't want to take advantage of your new boss."

"He won't mind," Shane said. "People like the Reveres and Dr. Prentice are his typical clients. An invite to the dinner and the wedding provides him with new contacts for PRESS."

"Okay, Josh is in. But I also want you to have a date—a real-live female date."

"You're talking about the French baker," he said. "The

way you're pushing her worries me. What's wrong with this woman?"

"Absolutely nothing. Marie has a sexy accent, a beautiful smile and great big blue eyes. She's tall and leggy and—"

"How tall?" he asked suspiciously. "Over eight feet? Does she have robins nesting in her hair?"

"Don't be a jerk."

"Does she even have hair?"

"Picky, picky, picky."

"Ha! I guessed it. You're trying to fix me up with a blue-eyed, bald giantess who bakes croissants."

She rolled her eyes. "No wonder you're still single."

"Nothing wrong with waiting for the right woman to come along." He sipped his wine and leaned back in his chair. "This is nice. You and me. Sitting here and relaxing."

"Very nice."

"I hate to bring up the stalker," he said.

"Then don't." She didn't want to face the possibility of a psycho stalker or the pre-nup or the endless details of her wedding. "Can't we just be normal people who chat about movies or books?"

"You're not normal, Angela. Like it or not, you're outstanding. Special."

His words tickled her memory. *She was special.* With all these other distractions, she'd almost forgotten about Dr. Prentice and his great big secret.

"Shane, do you remember when Tom first started talking about the frozen embryos?"

He arched an eyebrow. "What made you think of that?"

"Something Prentice said." Resting her elbows on the table, she leaned toward him. "I remember that Tom came home after a training session at the Army Medical Center, and he was all excited about having our embryos frozen."

"He'd heard a lecture from Prentice—something about biological warfare and the dangers of infection in the field. It scared the hell out of Tom. He was afraid he might come home sterile or put your future children in danger of some kind of genetic mutation."

"And he insisted on having the procedure done by Prentice even though the long trips to Aspen were inconvenient."

She'd been working as a sous-chef at an upscale French restaurant, and the head chef was a tyrant who complained about everything. Getting out from under his thumb wasn't easy, but she'd enjoyed the trips to Aspen, especially since they'd always stopped off to visit with Shane in Clear Creek County. After Tom deployed, Shane had actually taken her to the last appointment with Prentice.

"Anyway," she said, "Prentice ran my DNA. It seems that I was part of a study he did on an Army base in New Mexico. Twenty-six years ago, Prentice did the IVF procedure on several couples. Their children were supposed to be monitored throughout their lives, but my family dropped out."

"The Prentice-Jantzen study," Shane said. "You were one of those babies?"

"How do you know about it?"

"I ran a background check on Prentice while we were at PRESS. There was a recent murder related to the study, and some accusations of fraud. Prentice created embryos from high achievers. The babies were genetically engineered and didn't share the DNA of the mother and father who raised them." He drained the wine from his glass and poured more. "And you're a part of that study. Jeez, Angela, you're turning into some kind of trouble magnet."

"Neil thinks it makes me interesting," she said. "Plus, I have genius DNA. Maybe that's why Benjy is so bright."

"How does it make you feel? You weren't genetically related to your mother and father."

She shrugged. She might have been more disturbed if her father hadn't died when she was too young to know him. When her mother remarried, she had no genetic connection to her stepfather and hadn't bonded with him at all. They exchanged Christmas cards, but she hadn't seen him since her mother passed away eight years ago. When she wrote and told him she was getting married, he'd sent a congratulations card and fifty bucks. "My DNA doesn't seem all that important."

"Prentice lied to you." His voice deepened to a serious tone. Even though Shane was changing jobs, he had a lawman's stern morality. Lying was *always* wrong. "He didn't tell your parents that you weren't their biological child. And he never told you. That's fraud."

"It's not so black and white."

"You're defending him."

"I'm not saying what he did was right," she explained. "But my mother and father couldn't have a child, and Prentice made it possible. My mom carried me, gave birth to me and loved me as her only daughter. Who cares if our DNA didn't match?"

Though he sat motionless, she saw turmoil in his eyes as he tried to reconcile her opinion with the facts. In Shane's book, Prentice had committed a criminal act and deserved to be punished.

Usually, she trusted his opinion when it came to sorting out the good guys and bad guys. But how could she condemn Prentice? In a way, he was responsible for giving her Benjy.

"All the same," Shane said, "I'm keeping my eye on Prentice. I don't trust him."

"Once again, we'll agree to disagree. I think Prentice is a kindly old gent, and you think he's—"

"Up to no good." He pushed back from the table and stood. "Let's get back to the more immediate problem—namely, the stalker."

She rose to face him. "We seem to be jumping from one unpleasant situation to another. At least we see eye to eye on the stalker. He's definitely a bad guy."

"I can tell you that he's a lot more clever than I initially thought. And he's been here before."

A shiver trickled down her spine. "Watching me?"

"I don't want to speculate on what he's doing. It's easier if I show you."

The first stop was the guestroom where Shane would be sleeping tonight. He brought her inside and closed the door so their conversation wouldn't wake her sleeping child.

"First off," he said, "you need to remember that all the windows and doors are equipped with motion sensors. If you open one from the inside or the outside, an alarm goes off."

She'd heard the screaming banshee alarm when he and Benjy were installing the security system. "How do I turn it off?"

"There's a remote panel mounted by the front door. The code is Benjy's birthday."

"I can remember that."

"Over there is a monitor." He pointed to the dresser where a rectangular box with a screen sat amid a tangle of wires. "Go ahead and take a look."

On the split screen were black-and-white videos—a view of the front of her house and another that showed the back-yard. "You set up surveillance cameras."

"High-def cameras with infrared night vision that ensures we'll be able to identify anybody sneaking around. The equipment Josh uses is about a hundred times better than the Clear Creek County traffic cams. Benjy thinks it's pretty great."

"Me, too. It feels like I'm in a spy movie."

"It's supposed to make you feel safe."

She turned and faced him. Her big, broad-shouldered friend was a formidable man. There wasn't a stalker alive who'd want to mess with Shane. "The reason I feel safe is you."

"Aw, shucks, ma'am."

He grinned, and for a moment she felt a spark of attraction that was totally inappropriate for a woman who was about to be married to another. Quickly, she looked away. "What did you need to show me about the stalker?"

"After I set up the alarm system, I swept your whole house for bugs. In here, I found something."

He opened the kneehole drawer on the small desk under the window, reached inside and took out a small disc. "This bug does more than listen. It allows for two-way transmissions."

The disc—no bigger than a nickel—looked harmless but the implication horrified her. The stalker had been monitoring her, invading the privacy of her home. "Shouldn't we throw it away?"

"I've already disabled the device," he said. "It's nothing high-tech. You could probably pick it up online. I'm guessing that the effective range for this bug is only about a hundred yards. Your stalker could have been parked on the street, listening."

"What was he trying to hear?"

"He also planted one of these devices in your bedroom," Shane said, "but not in the kitchen or the front room. That makes me think that he wanted to hear your nighttime routine. He'd wait until after you put Benjy down for the night, after you took a shower and turned off the television. He'd know when you went to bed."

The hairs on the back of her neck prickled. She'd had no idea. When she read stories to Benjy or sang in the shower, when she curled up in bed and sighed, when she whispered to herself, he'd been listening.

Shane continued, "After you were asleep, he'd use the speaker function. He could make a loud noise from this room. Or he might use the speaker in your bedroom to talk to you."

"Why? What would he say?"

"It doesn't matter. The purpose was to keep you from getting a good night's rest."

She sank down on the twin bed in the guestroom. Though she couldn't exactly pinpoint the time when her edginess started, it was probably a couple of weeks ago when the wedding plans went into high gear. Being tired seemed normal; there was so much to do. But there were plenty of times she'd awakened in the night for no apparent reason. "I thought I was losing my mind."

"You were sleep-deprived. An effective torture technique."

"Shane, are you certain about this?"

"Come with me." He opened the door, and they tiptoed down the hallway to her bedroom where he again closed them in so Benjy wouldn't be disturbed. "Lie down on the bed."

She did as he said, watching as he reached up to the frame above the door. "What are you doing?"

"I'm operating this manually, but your stalker used a remote."

When he turned off the overhead light, she saw a flash

from above the doorframe. Like a flashlight beam, it aimed at her head on the pillow. She bolted from the bed. "Turn it off."

He flicked the overhead light switch. "If the noises didn't wake you up, he could activate this nasty little spotlight."

"And he could have timed it perfectly," she said. "Waking me up at ten twenty-three. I'd look at the clock. Think of Tom. My God, no wonder I thought I was going crazy."

"Seems to me," Shane said, "that the stalker's motive in doing all this was to terrorize you. He took pleasure in watching you fall apart. The slashed wedding gown should have been the last straw—the final act that sent you over the edge."

If Shane hadn't been with her when she saw that gown, she might have crashed and burned. She remembered the vertigo, the shortness of breath and the devastating fear that she'd destroyed the dress herself. "Who would do this to me? Why?"

"I don't have that answer," he said, "but I have a solution. Now that you know what's going on, you don't have to doubt yourself. There's not a damn thing wrong with you."

Except that a psycho stalker had targeted her. "What should I do?"

"Tonight, you get a solid eight hours of sleep. Tomorrow, you act with your usual confidence. Your stalker can't scare you anymore. He's lost. You've won."

This moment didn't feel like a victory. Someone hated her enough to rig up this elaborate scheme. He'd been lurking outside her house. Listening to her. Watching her stumble deeper into emotional distress.

"What do you think he'll do next? Am I in danger?" An even more terrible thought occurred to her. "Would he try to hurt Benjy?"

"I'll keep you safe. Both of you." Shane rested his large, reassuring hand on her shoulder. "Tonight, your job is to sleep. Since you know what's going on, you don't need a sedative. Right?"

She looked up at him. He hadn't directly accused Neil, but she knew what he was thinking. Shane had insisted that her prescription be analyzed.

"I won't take a pill tonight," she said. "But I want to be clear about one thing. Neil couldn't have done this. He's a busy man and wouldn't have had time to sneak around outside my house. Besides, stalking isn't the kind of thing he'd do."

"Because it's low class," Shane drawled. "Did you know that Jack the Ripper—a serial killer who disemboweled prostitutes on the streets of London—might have been related to the royal family? Evidence suggests he was a medical man."

"Seriously. You're not really comparing Neil to Jack the Ripper?"

"Until I know better, I suspect everybody," he said. "That includes your fiancé, his father and the housekeeper who made that pitiful lunch."

"Is there a way to narrow down that list?"

"With a stalker, it's difficult. He could be somebody who you don't even notice. Like a regular customer at Waffles or another shopkeeper or the guy who delivers packages. In his mind, he might have built up a fantasy relationship with you. An obsession."

"Why?"

"Some guys get crazy ideas in their heads," Shane said. "The important thing for you to know is that you didn't do anything to cause this. It's not your fault."

The idea of a stranger being obsessed with her was more frightening than if she knew who had set up this elaborate scheme. She was already regretting her promise not to take a sedative before bed. "How am I going to sleep?"

"There's nothing to be scared of," he said. "I'm here, and I'll keep you safe."

She believed him—believed *in* him.

Chapter Ten

The next day, all day, Shane acted as Angela's bodyguard. He wore his gun in a shoulder holster that was unnoticeable under his blazer and hid the tension in his gaze behind a pair of dark sunglasses. Though he didn't expect a straight-forward attack from her stalker, he was prepared.

Protecting her might have been easier if she hadn't gotten a decent rest the night before. Angela was operating at full throttle, fielding dozens of phone calls and finalizing wedding arrangements. With Shane driving her van, they went from Waffles to the florist shop to the bakery where he finally met Marie Devereaux, who was as pretty as Angela had promised. Her black hair and blue eyes almost matched his coloring, and her smokey voice, lightly tinged with a French accent, was sexy and charming. He should have been attracted to her, but he felt nothing when he shook her hand. No spark.

At four o'clock, they dropped Benjy off with the babysitter where he would spend the night, and they returned to her house so Angela could get ready for the rehearsal and the dinner at the private dining room in Neil's country club. Shane's preparations for the evening took only a couple of minutes. He changed from his plaid cotton shirt to a white one with a button-down collar and dusted off the toes of his boots. His jeans were okay for tonight; the dinner wasn't supposed to be formal.

Sitting in her living room, he waited. Josh LaMotta and the lovely Marie would meet them here, and they'd all drive north together.

Shane looked forward to the chance to talk with Josh and review the evidence. With insights from his new boss, he might be able to come up with answers; there had to be a better theory than what he was thinking now. But facts didn't lie and the pattern was obvious: Neil's custody demands in the pre-nup were designed to take Benjy away from his mother if she suffered a nervous breakdown, and her stalker used sleep deprivation to send her into a downward emotional spiral. The two events had to be connected.

Logic told him that Neil was behind the stalking, but he had no hard evidence. Not yet, anyway.

Angela emerged from her bedroom, checking her wristwatch and looking very nice in a gauzy light green dress with a thick belt that made her waist look tiny. Her thick brown hair was pulled back in a French braid that fell halfway down her back. Even though she was wearing platform sandals, she moved fast.

"We need to leave pretty soon," she said. "I don't want to be late to the chapel."

"Relax. They can't start without the bride."

"Are you sure Josh knows where I live?"

"He found his way down from Mount Elbert with nothing but a compass. I think he can make it from the Tech Center to your house." He stood and took her hand. All he really wanted was for her to be happy. If that meant marrying Neil, Shane would step aside like a gentleman. "You look great."

"Do you think I need more makeup?"

He hadn't noticed that she was wearing anything other than a bit of color on her lips. "You're perfect."

"And the dress? Not too plain, is it?"

In her eyes, he noticed a shadow, a hint that all was not right. "Something bothering you?"

"I don't know." Her slender shoulders rose and fell in a shrug. "I can't stop thinking about the pre-nup. And the stalker."

"Me, too."

"These things don't just happen. Somehow, I must have brought this on myself."

"You haven't done anything wrong." *Except getting involved with Neil.* He wanted to point the finger of suspicion, but the more he condemned her fiancé, the more she defended him.

"You always support me." Her pink lips curved in a grin. "I liked having you with me today."

"A free bodyguard. Not a bad deal."

The doorbell rang. Shane deactivated the alarm system, and opened the door for Josh and Marie, who had arrived simultaneously and were chatting. *In French.*

AT THE SMALL STONE CHAPEL in the foothills outside Golden, Shane positioned himself near the arched entryway and watched as the wedding party assembled on the grass. He was still wearing his sunglasses, still on alert.

After Josh seated Marie inside with the others, he took a position next to Shane. They were almost the same height, but Josh was as lean as a greyhound, which was ironic because he ate constantly—an appetite he blamed on his pasta-pushing Italian grandmother who made the best meatballs west of the Mississippi. He asked, "How was your day as a bodyguard?"

"Good practice." Not that he needed training. From his

years as a deputy, Shane had learned how to recognize trouble before it erupted. Being a bodyguard was second nature. "I couldn't ID anybody as the stalker."

"What were you looking for?"

There was a lot Josh could teach him in terms of technical skills and equipment, but Shane was confident in some abilities. He drawled, "I was kind of hoping for a name tag. You know, a badge that says, Hello, I'm a Psycho."

"Sarcasm?"

"This isn't my first ride on the merry-go-round. You know what I was looking for. Signals of lying. Furtive behavior. Inappropriate responses." All day, he'd been watching and analyzing. "Angela interacts with a lot of people. None came across as suspicious."

"And you got nothing from the security cams you set up at the house?"

"I checked the replay this morning. *Nada.*"

A portly little pastor bustled around, organizing the small procession. Neil would be waiting at the altar. Benjy, the ring bearer, and the daughter of the best man would come first. Since neither of the kids were here, Yvonne would be in charge of starting them down the aisle, after which she and the best man would enter. The bridal march would play and Angela would enter, escorted by Shane.

He didn't want to give her away. Tension clenched inside his chest. This wedding shouldn't be taking place.

"Can you take a bit of professional advice?" Josh asked.

"I guess."

"When you're working a small event like this, the client might want you to stand out so everybody knows there's a bodyguard present. Or they might want you to fit in. I'm guessing that Angela wants the latter."

"I'm fitting in."

"You're about as subtle as a fist. Quit flexing."

But Shane wanted Neil to know he was there, wanted to post a signpost that warned Neil, his father and Prentice that he was protecting Angela. "Since Angela is my client, I have an agenda of my own."

Josh nodded. "How long have you been in love with her?"

"We're friends. She was married to my cousin."

"Whatever you say." His dark eyes were far too perceptive. "In any case, I couldn't help but notice that you and Marie aren't exactly hitting it off."

"The mademoiselle is all yours."

"Merci beaucoup."

Shane scanned from the jagged foothills that rose behind them to the uncultivated acreage to the east. Though they'd had plenty of moisture this summer, the rolling hills had faded to a dull khaki with occasional green. He wasn't in love with Angela. Sure, he cared about her. And sometimes when he caught a sudden glimpse or her or saw her from far away, his chest got tight and he found it hard to breathe. Sure, he'd wondered what would have happened if he'd met Angela first, before his cousin. But it hadn't happened that way, and he'd be a fool to pine away with some kind of hopeless attraction to his cousin's widow.

His gaze focused on the group gathered in the small churchyard enclosed by a picket fence. Angela was talking to Yvonne, and their expressions were concerned. Probably talking about a problem at Waffles; Yvonne was going to have a rough time handling the restaurant on her own while Angela was on her two-week honeymoon in Baja.

Beyond the picket fence was a two-lane road. A line of traffic chugged past—two SUVs and a black truck. In the parking lot to the south, several vehicles were parked.

He looked toward Josh. "Now that you've met Neil, what's your read on him?"

"He's egotistical and self-important. His colleagues would say he has good cause. After all, he's a genius virologist who's saving the world from disease. Neil is the kind of man who needs to control everything. Hence, the custody section in the pre-nup. He's not somebody I'd choose to pal around with, but I'm trying to maintain a good opinion because Angela's marrying the guy and I like her."

"Do you think he's involved with the stalker?"

"He wouldn't do it himself," Josh said. "Wouldn't get his hands dirty."

"But he could hire someone."

"The big question is, Why? Even if Angela had signed the pre-nup, legal custody favors the natural mother. The court battles would go on for years."

So why did Neil want Benjy?

The pastor waved his hand, summoning Shane to take his position in the wedding procession. He came down the three wide stone steps and got into line.

Angela threaded her arm through his and shot him a grin. Under her breath, she said, "Were you paying attention?"

"Don't trip over my own feet. And don't walk too fast."

"Not complicated," she said.

The hard part would come after the ceremony started and the pastor asked if anyone objected to the marriage— the "Speak now or forever hold your peace" part. Shane objected. A lot.

IN THE PRIVATE DINING ROOM at Neil's country club, seventeen guests sat at two rectangular tables with white daisy centerpieces and brightly flickering candles. The French doors opened onto a deck with a view of a vast, green golf course.

Shane was seated at the head of the second table with Josh on one side and a plump, gray-haired woman who was an ob-gyn on the other. From his vantage point, he was able to observe most of the guests. In spite of his misgivings about the wedding, there was nothing sinister about this group that included a couple of employees from Waffles and colleagues who worked with Neil.

His gaze fixed on Angela. She was bright and vivacious, outshining Neil in every way. Her happy mood seemed to have started when they arrived at the country club and went into a private office where Josh read the revised pre-nup and she had written her signature with a flourish. As soon as she lifted the pen, a weight seemed to fall from her shoulders. By signing the prenuptial agreement, she was committed. There was no reason why the wedding shouldn't go forward.

Except for his suspicions.

He tried his best to put on a positive face. She was getting married. And he was supposed to be happy for her. Everybody else appeared to be having a good time. The meal started with a bite-size bit of pastry with blue cheese and an asparagus tip that Marie called an *amuse bouche.* "It's supposed to excite the palate," she said. "It gives the chef a way to show off."

The fancy tidbit made his stomach growl. The rest of the crowd tasted a red wine that was designed especially to complement the *bouche* thing, but he wasn't drinking. Not only was he driving home, but he wanted to keep his wits about him.

Leaning back in his chair, he tried not to scowl. There was nothing like being the only sober person in the room to make sure you had a dandy time.

Since Josh was occupied with chatting up the lovely Marie, Shane turned to the sweet-faced older woman beside him. "Dr. Davenport," he said, "how did you get to know Neil?"

"We met at the Army Medical Center. Actually, I'm much closer to Dr. Prentice," she said. "And please call me Emily."

"Okay, Emily." It occurred to him that instead of pretending to have fun, he could use this time to gather information. These rehearsal dinner guests could be suspects, after all. "Are you a fertility expert, like Prentice?"

"Heavens, no. Lab work isn't my thing. I'm a baby doc."

Her grandmotherly sweetness almost convinced him to stop his line of interrogation, but the clarity in her baby-blue eyes made him think that she might not view the world through rose-colored lenses. As a test, he offered a chance to gossip. "I understand that Dr. Prentice has had some legal troubles recently."

"He calls it genetic engineering, but I call it fraud." With an amiable smile, she added, "What the hell was he thinking?"

Apparently, this kindly, gray-haired lady had an edge. He leaned closer to her. "I don't know any of Neil's friends. Maybe you could fill me in."

According to Emily, the best man was on the same career track as Neil. Their supposed friendship was based on the theory of "Keep your enemies close." And the best man's wife—also a doctor—resented the time she took off from work to have her baby. "She's competitive. Little Benjy's intelligence threatens her, and she won't be friendly with Angela."

"Good to know," he said. "What about the young guy at the end of the table?"

"In spite of the baby face and the floppy brown hair, Jay Carlson isn't as young as he looks. Probably your age. Doesn't seem bright enough to have made it all the way through med school. Neil calls him a protégé, but uses him like a gofer. Carlson is the one who fetches the espresso drinks and tidies up the filing."

"He does Neil's dirty work," Shane said.

"Last summer, Carlson's main assignment was to build a gazebo in Neil's backyard."

"He has carpentry skills?"

"Which suit him a great deal better than the practice of medicine." Her deceptively sweet smile stayed in place. "The woman sitting opposite Carlson is a secretary at the med school. Blonde and bland and plain as mud. She has quite a crush on Neil."

The main course—beef Wellington—was served. While Shane was eating, he considered the protégé and the secretary. Either of them could have set out to terrorize Angela. The secretary might have been motivated by a desire to throw a wrench into the wedding. And Carlson could be doing more of Neil's dirty work.

Further chat with Emily revealed more of the harsh underbelly in Neil's supposedly idyllic world. It seemed that when these doctors weren't busy saving the world, they engaged in all kinds of nasty infighting. Every business had a dark side.

After their dinner plates were cleared and a custard dessert was passed around, he asked, "Tell me, Dr. Em, what do you like about your work?"

"I do it for the patients," she said simply. "Delivering babies makes me happy. I never set out to do research, but I stumbled over a genetic anomaly that gave me a big reputation."

"How big?"

She sipped her wine. "Enough that Neil and Prentice both want to be my best friend."

At the main table, Yvonne tapped her knife against her glass. "Attention, everybody."

Conversations stilled. The guests waited expectantly as Yvonne rose. In her high heels, she loomed over six feet tall. Her dress was an explosion of pink and purple. "After the wedding ceremony," she said, "it'll be time for toasts. But I thought it might be nice if we shared a few memories about the happy couple. I'll start."

Of course, her memory centered on Waffles. "The first time I met Neil, he showed up for breakfast. I knew he and Angela were dating so when he ordered an egg-white omelet, I ignored his request and brought him a praline waffle."

Yvonne nodded as everyone who had tasted Angela's finest recipe murmured with remembered bliss. She continued, "Neil ate the whole thing. I'm pretty sure that's when he fell in love."

Several other people offered comments. Neil's father blustered through a generic speech about gaining a daughter and a grandson. He never mentioned Neil's mother. Nobody talked about her, and the omission might be significant.

Dr. Prentice talked about Benjy and his dinosaurs.

Marie raised her wineglass and recited a love poem in French while Josh looked on adoringly.

Since Shane didn't really have any memories of Neil and Angela as a couple, he made a quick comment about how proud he was to be escorting the bride down the aisle.

Then, it was Emily's turn. "I remember," she said, "the first time Angela and Neil met. Six years ago. It was at the Army Medical Center where Angela volunteered and always brought the most delectable treats. She was in one of the common rooms, talking to injured soldiers. Most of the boys called her Angel."

Shane remembered how proud Tom had been of his wife and her volunteering. Everybody loved Angela.

Emily continued, "Neil passed by in the hallway. He came to a halt when he saw her. From the way he looked at her, I could tell that he wanted this lovely Angel for his own."

Even though she'd been married to another man. Shane swallowed his bitterness. From the start, Neil wanted to own her. Not to love her or cherish her. To him, Angela was just another possession.

Chapter Eleven

Today is my wedding day. Angela couldn't have asked for better weather—warm summer sunshine and clear, blue, Colorado skies. A good omen, she hoped.

In spite of the heavy meal last night, she got a solid eight hours' sleep, uninterrupted by the midnight whispers of her stalker, and she was absolutely bursting with energy. Rather than pace in circles for the next four hours before they needed to depart for the ceremony, she decided to get outside for a run. It was a perfect time; Benjy was with the babysitter.

Though she preferred jogging alone, Shane was still acting as her bodyguard and insisted on coming with. "Fine," she said, "as long as you don't bring your gun."

"No problem. I'll change."

Moments later, he emerged from the guest bedroom wearing a sleeveless T-shirt and baggy shorts. With his black hair uncombed and his jaw textured with stubble, he looked more like an urban guy who shot hoops than a deputy from Silver Plume.

She stared at his black running shoes. "I don't think I've ever seen you without your boots. You didn't used to work out."

"Nope."

"But now you do?"

He keyed the code numbers into the pad beside the front door and stepped outside. "There's a lot about me you don't know."

Since there wasn't much traffic, they jogged next to the cars parked at the curb. Her usual route—2.8 miles—looped through her neighborhood to a nearby park and back home again.

She set an easygoing pace. The steady rhythm felt good. She used to make this run every day after work as a way of winding down and shifting gears before she picked up her son, but her routine had been disrupted by the wedding preparations. She missed this physical activity. When her body was moving, her mind had a chance to reflect.

Today is my wedding day. From now on, this date would be circled on the calendar and celebrated in anniversaries. A special date. A date to be remembered.

She and Tom would have been married six years on the twelfth of November. It seemed so long ago. She'd been only twenty—young but not naive. She knew their marriage faced significant obstacles. His deployment into combat zones was one. His alcoholism, another. Though he'd stopped drinking, the issue was always present. They'd argued and struggled, but she had never, ever doubted their love.

She glanced over at Shane. "Tired?"

"Not me. You?"

"I feel great."

To prove it, she sprinted toward the corner house with the rows of yellow and purple pansies bordering the sidewalk. The garage door had been recently painted the same yellow as the cheerful flowers. On the next block, she saw two "For Sale" signs, like the one on her house. A pang of regret tightened her stride; she didn't want to leave. Her cozy neighborhood was nowhere near as upscale as Neil's, but she loved living here.

At the edge of the park, she slowed to a walk and caught her breath. The smell of freshly mown grass refreshed her senses. There were no children on the playground equipment surrounded by sand, so she went to one of the swings and sat. "I'm going to miss this."

"I'm sure Neil would buy you a jungle gym."

"Not the playground. This neighborhood. My house. All of this. My normal life."

He went behind her, hooked his hands through the chains and pulled her way back. When he gave a push, she went soaring. The toes of her running shoes pointed to the sky.

She kept her legs straight, and he pushed again. Her head tilted back; she was airborne.

Simple pleasures were the best. A run on a sunlit day. The sound of laughter. The aroma of a fresh-baked apple pie. Neil could give her emeralds and diamonds. He could send Benjy to the best schools and probably arrange for her son to go to Harvard. But would he play with her on a swing set?

It was an unfair question. She dragged her feet to stop. The love she felt for Neil wasn't like the fireworks with Tom or her friendship with Shane. Her relationship with Neil was mature and solid. Grounded.

Hopping off the swing, she turned toward Shane. She'd always been able to tell him anything, but talking about Neil was impossible. Shane hated her fiancé. He suspected him of being involved with the stalker and drugging her.

She launched into a different subject. "Looks like you're not going to have a date for the wedding reception. Marie was supposed to fall for you, but she and Josh hit it off."

He clutched his chest. "Shot down again."

"Oh, please." She'd seen how women reacted to this big, handsome mountain man and doubted that he got rejected often.

"For your information, I do have a date. Dr. Emily."

The sweet, little, gray-haired ob-gyn? "Huh? I never took her for a cougar."

"I like older women." He grinned. "The older, the better."

"Last night, when everybody was talking about their memories, I was surprised by what Emily had to say. Of course, I remember meeting Neil at the Army Medical Center, but I had no idea he'd seen me earlier and sought me out."

"Like a predator."

"Stop casting him in a bad light. Neil knew that I was married. He met Tom. They talked about anthrax." He hadn't chased her at all. Their relationship had developed gradually, over a period of years. "What else did Emily say?"

"She warned me about the best man and his wife. A super-competitive couple, they aren't going to be good friends, especially not if Benjy outshines their daughter."

Though Angela wasn't big on gossip, she knew that one of her wifely duties would be to attend events with Neil and entertain his colleagues. It was important to know what to expect. "Anything else?"

"Dr. Em doesn't like Carlson, Neil's protégé."

On this count, Angela agreed. "Neither do I. He's kind of creepy."

"Like a stalker?"

"I hope not." But Carlson sent out that kind of vibe. A couple of times, she'd caught him watching her with a little smirk on his face. "I don't think he'd do anything to jeopardize his mentor-student relationship. He worships Neil."

"And if Neil suggested the stalk—"

"We need to get back to the house." She wouldn't listen to another negative word about Neil. Turning away, she started jogging around the park.

Shane ran beside her. "You have to face the possibility."

"Can't hear you."

She picked up the pace, refusing to be drawn into vague speculation. Shane's dislike for Neil didn't translate into some kind of plot to drive her crazy and get custody of Benjy. Unless there was proof... Unless the tests on the sedatives he gave her showed something different...

All she wanted was to be married and happy. To make a good life for her son. To have some security.

Today is my wedding day.

THOUGH YVONNE CAME OVER to help Angela get ready for the wedding, there really wasn't much to do. The cream-colored silk suit fit perfectly, and she'd already decided to wear her long hair up. The only question was the pouffy net veil that would have been totally appropriate with the gown but looked silly with a suit. She pinned it on the top of her head. "I look like a cockatoo."

"I never got the point of wearing a veil," Yvonne said. "The groom already knows what the bride looks like so when he picks it up, there's no big shock. Unless you paint on a fake moustache."

"Or not." She tried the veil on the back of her head. "Maybe when I get to the chapel, I'll just stick a daisy from the bouquet into my hair."

Benjy came into her bedroom. In his little blue blazer

and necktie, he was utterly adorable. "Mommy, I don't want you to get married."

"And why is that?"

"You're going away with Neil."

"I'll be back before you know it." She didn't want to be apart from Benjy for two whole weeks, but taking a child on her honeymoon wasn't exactly key to a romantic relationship with her new husband.

"Hey, Benjy." When Yvonne squatted down to talk to him, the skirt of her forest-green sheath stretched tight across her bottom. "I'm going to miss your mom, too. But we'll have fun while she's gone. One day, I'll take you to the museum to see the dinosaur bones."

He held up two fingers. "Two times."

"Twice it is. And the zoo."

"We're going to the zoo," Benjy said. "I'm going to tell Shane. He can come with us."

As he ran from the room, Angela flung the veil onto her bed. A trip to the zoo with Shane and Benjy sounded like a hundred times more fun than the wedding ceremony. She looked into the mirror one last time and practiced her smile. She didn't look happy.

"You're gorgeous," Yvonne said. "A beautiful bride."

"I never wanted this big ceremony. It's too much."

Her friend shrugged. "You ought to make a good haul on wedding gifts."

"We already have too much stuff. Everything from my house will have to go into storage."

"You're not selling your things?"

"I probably should." The worn furniture she'd chosen with care would never look right in Neil's house.

Yvonne checked her wristwatch. "We're just about ready. Shane has everything packed. He shifted Benjy's car seat into the back of his Land Rover. And his bags. And your carry-on with the cosmetics."

Shane tapped on the open door before he entered. "Yvonne, would you watch Benjy? I need to talk to Angela alone."

"Sure thing, but we need to get moving." She tapped her wristwatch. "Ticktock."

As soon as she bustled out the door, he closed it. "I heard from the lab. They analyzed the pills Neil prescribed for you."

The air went out of her lungs. She sank down on the bed. "Tell me."

"Not sedatives," he said. "They're mild stimulants with hallucinogenic properties."

"What does that mean?" She had a pretty good idea, but didn't want to believe it. "When I took a pill, what would happen?"

"Your heart rate would accelerate. You sure as hell wouldn't be able to sleep. Your perceptions would be altered. The pills triggered your panic attacks."

"Are you sure?"

"I can show you the lab report." He knelt before her and took her hands. "I'm sorry, Angela."

Neil lied to her. All his supposedly considerate attention was a sham. How could he have done this to her? She'd thought she was losing her mind. She almost let him railroad her into seeing a psychiatrist.

Looking into Shane's gentle blue eyes, she saw pity. "Don't feel sorry for me. I got myself into this mess, and I'll get myself out."

"You're not alone," he said. "Whatever you decide, I'm here to help."

She pulled her hands away from his grasp and stood. Renewed energy coursed through her body. There was only one thing to do. In a tight voice, she said, "Excuse me, please. I need to make a phone call."

"I'll wait right outside the door."

She watched the door close, went to the dresser and picked up the outrageously expensive beaded white clutch purse that Neil had bought for her. Inside was a lipstick, a pocket holding her driver's license and ATM card, a comb and her cell phone. She dumped the contents into her usual shoulder bag that was full of the necessities of her life as a single mother and business owner. Her real identity didn't include fancy purses and big houses and oversize weddings. She should have known.

Neil's engagement ring glinted on her finger. She hardly ever wore it. The ring got in her way when she was cooking, and she was afraid of losing the pear-shaped diamond when she was chasing after Benjy. She never should have said yes to Neil's proposal.

She picked up the cell phone and hit speed dial.

Neil answered right away. "It's a beautiful day for a wedding," he said. "Are you on your way?"

"You drugged me."

"What are you talking about?"

"I had the blue pills analyzed. You wanted me to think I was having panic attacks."

"A misunderstanding." His voice turned cold. "We'll talk about it after the ceremony. The chapel is filled with daisies. It's magnificent."

"I won't marry you, Neil."

A silence widened the gulf between them. There was nothing he could say to change her mind. Not only had he attacked her sanity but his motives threatened her son. She'd never put Benjy in danger.

"Angela, be reasonable. Our guests are arriving. The

wedding gifts have been sent. Everything is ready and waiting for you."

A wave of anger washed over her. "Did you really think that I'd fall apart? That I'd ever be so far gone that I would give up my son? Leave him in your custody?"

"If you really cared about Benjy, you'd want him to have all the advantages I can provide."

You bastard! "The wedding is off."

"I'm warning you, Angela. I won't let you humiliate me like this."

"Goodbye, Neil."

She disconnected the call. It was over. In spite of twinges of guilt and shame, she felt an overwhelming sense of relief. Thanks to Shane's suspicions, she had avoided the worst mistake of her life.

And she knew exactly what she needed to do next. Flinging open the door, she faced Shane. "Benjy and I are coming to stay with you for a couple of weeks."

"You called off your wedding."

"In the nick of time."

He wrapped her in a hug, and she held on tight. Once again, he'd come riding to her rescue.

"You're doing the right thing," he assured her. "Throw some of your clothes and Benjy's into a bag, and we'll get the hell out of here."

With no time for careful packing, she threw clothes into big, black garbage bags.

Yvonne appeared to help. As she dumped the contents of Angela's underwear drawer into the bag, she said, "I couldn't say this before, but I never liked Neil. I'm glad you're not marrying him."

"Really?"

"He's the most condescending man I've ever seen. A lot of doctors are like that, but Neil is the worst." She slung the bag over her shoulder like Santa Claus. "Stay in touch, but don't worry about the restaurant. I've got it covered."

Within ten minutes of her phone call to Neil, they were packed and driving away from her house. From the backseat, Benjy asked, "Where are we going?"

"To the mountains," Shane replied.

"Can I ride horses?"

"You bet."

When he pulled up at the stop sign on the corner, a silver SUV purposely drove in front of them and stopped, blocking their way. She should have known that Neil wouldn't let her go without a fight.

Chapter Twelve

Shane had expected trouble, but not so soon. They hadn't even gotten a block away from her house before facing a confrontation. Given a choice, Shane preferred to stand and fight. But not this time. First and foremost, he needed to get Angela and her son to a safe place.

From the backseat, Benjy piped up, "Why aren't we going?"

"This guy is a bad driver," Shane said. "It's no big deal. I'll talk to him. Maybe I should write him a ticket."

Benjy asked, "Can I come with you?"

In unison, he and Angela said, "No."

As he opened the car door, she shifted around in her seat to talk to her son. In her white suit with her hair all done up on top of her head, she looked formal and controlled. The only sign of tension was the flush of red that colored her slender throat and dotted her cheeks.

He strode toward the driver's side of the SUV. Though the window, he saw Carlson. Though Dr. Em had told him this guy was in his thirties, he looked like a rebellious teenager with his brown hair flopping over his forehead, hiding his eyes. His jaw nervously worked a piece of gum.

When Shane tapped on the glass, he buzzed it down. Through tight lips, Carlson said, "Neil wants me to drive Angela to the wedding."

"And you happen to be so close. It's almost like you've been spying on us."

His jaw stopped moving. "Why would I do that?"

"You like watching Angela." *Stalking her.* "Can't say as I blame you. She's a good-looking woman."

"Not my type." The words exploded from his mouth.

"Oh, I think she is. I think you've got a thing for her. And that could be a problem for you, Carlson. Neil wouldn't like it if you made a play for his bride. He might not want to be your mentor, and you could find yourself out of a job."

He chewed more vigorously as though he could draw strength from his gum. "That's not how it is. Neil wants me here, keeping an eye on things."

"You're just following orders."

"Damn right."

He sounded as if he was boasting. Dr. Em had been right in her assessment of Carlson's intelligence—not bright enough to be a doctor. He seemed barely clever enough to tie his own shoes. "Tell me, Carlson. Were you the one who planted the bugs in Angela's house? Or did Neil do that himself?"

"You don't know anything. You've got no evidence."

At the moment, he wasn't trying to build a legal case. His primary objective was to get Angela and Benjy out of town. "Here's one thing I know for certain. Neil is real fond of Benjy. That's true, isn't it?"

"Yeah," Carlson said suspiciously.

"He wouldn't want you to upset the kid. Right?"

He nodded.

Shane pulled his arm back, offering a clear view of his shoulder holster. He had no intention of using his gun, but he wanted Carlson to see the threat.

"Here's what's going to happen," Shane said. "I'll get back in my car and tell Benjy there's nothing wrong. Then

I'm going to drive away safely, following all the rules of the road."

"But they're supposed to ride with me."

"You can follow me. Drive safely. We don't want to put Benjy in a high-speed chase, do we?"

His gum chewing paused. He pursed his lips in a pouty expression that would have been unappealing on a woman. On a man, it was downright disgusting. "I guess not."

"We have an understanding." Shane patted the side of the car. "You pull out of my way, and we won't have any trouble."

As he stepped away from the SUV, he saw Carlson hold his cell phone to his ear. No doubt, he was getting his instructions from Neil.

Shane slid into the driver's seat of his Land Rover. If Carlson didn't move, he could drive down the block in reverse and make a clear getaway. But he preferred the simpler solution. He turned to Angela. "I think we have this straightened out."

"Should I call 911?"

"Nine-one-one," Benjy parroted. "911."

They were going to need backup, but Shane didn't want to bring in law enforcement. The police would be required to detain them and take statements, which meant that Neil would have time to get here. Angela's ex-fiancé would be a hell of a lot harder to deal with than his sidekick.

Carlson's SUV pulled forward, leaving their route unobstructed.

"We're just fine," he said. "Everybody buckled up?"

"I am," Benjy said cheerfully. "You know what? Mommy isn't taking a honeymoon. She's going to stay with me."

"In the mountains," Angela said.

Her gaze slid toward the sideview mirror. Though apprehensive, she didn't seem scared. Either she was putting on a brave face for Benjy or she was honestly unafraid. He hoped for the latter, hoped that she realized that calling off the wedding was the right move.

As he drove away from her neighborhood onto a main road, he glanced in the rearview mirror. Carlson's SUV hung on their tail, making no attempt to be subtle.

Shane had expected as much. He clipped his hands-free phone onto his ear and called Josh, who could provide all the backup he needed.

"Where are we headed?" Angela asked.

"The PRESS building."

"Yay," Benjy called out. "Can we go to the lab and look in the microscope?"

"Not today," Shane said.

"Neil has microscopes in his lab," Benjy said. "But he never lets me touch. Germs are very little. You can't see them unless you look real close."

"Not like dinosaurs."

"T-Rex is very big."

Shane used his signal lights and gave Carlson plenty of room to change lanes. His objective was to have the silver SUV trail him into the parking lot outside the PRESS building in the Tech Center. Following Josh's instructions, he drove around to the rear of the building where there was only one lane between the sidewalk and a row of parked cars.

He spotted Josh standing near the end of the sidewalk. Josh pointed, and Shane made a sudden sharp turn into a parking slot. Carlson stopped, not knowing which way to go.

At a signal from Josh, two PRESS vehicles moved into place—one at the front of the silver SUV and one behind. Carlson was trapped.

Josh jogged over to the Land Rover and looked in the

window. "It's a damn good thing I like you because you're turning into a major troublemaker."

Angela leaned over and said, "I'm so sorry for the inconvenience."

"Protecting you is good exercise." Josh grinned. "To tell you the truth, these guys are happy to have something to do other than desk work."

The "guys" Josh referred to included four of his employees who left their vehicles and took positions on both sides of the SUV. All wore dark glasses. Two wore dark blazers, and the other two had on knit golf shirts, also black, that showed off chiseled biceps when they folded their arms across their chests. These were men of action who worked out regularly in the PRESS gym. Not even Carlson was dumb enough to mess with them.

With obvious deference, he climbed out of the SUV and asked them to move their vehicles, please. When they didn't respond, he stared down at his toes and shuffled nervously.

Shane said to Josh, "I appreciate the backup."

"I aim to please."

"Give us fifteen minutes before you let him go."

"You got it."

Without warning, Angela flung open her door. Before Shane had a chance to object, she charged across the asphalt toward the silver SUV.

As soon as Carlson saw her, he darted toward her and waved. "Over here, Angela. You're supposed to come with me."

Carlson's "guys" stepped up to intervene, but Angela halted them with an upraised palm. "I can handle this."

From the backseat, Benjy asked, "What's Mommy doing?"

"Taking care of business," Shane said.

He watched as she and Carlson faced off. They stood about fifteen feet away from him. His hand rested on the door handle, ready to leap out if she required assistance.

"Hold out your hand," she said to Carlson. "Palm up."

"If you get in the car," he said, "we can still make it to the wedding on time. We can pretend this never hap—"

"Your hand," she snapped.

He did as she said.

She twisted the engagement ring off her finger and slapped it into his open palm. "Return this to Neil. I don't want to ever see it again."

He stared at the glittering diamond as though it was a scorpion. When he looked at her, anger twisted his features. "You ungrateful bitch, you can't treat Neil like this. Not after everything he's done for you."

"I don't owe him a thing." Though she kept her voice low, Shane heard every word. "Not after his lies. And the drugs. And the stalking. He tried to make me think I was insane."

"Didn't have to try too hard, did he?" Carlson sneered. "You're crazy. You can't call off the wedding."

"But I just did."

When she reached over and patted Carlson on the cheek, Shane swore he could see flames shooting from her eyes. Angela pivoted on the delicate heel of her white bridal shoe and stalked back to the car.

Carlson yelled at her departing back. "Neil is never going to let you go. Never."

Shane took the threat seriously. Neil and his minions had gone to a lot of trouble arranging this setup, and they wouldn't allow Angela to simply walk away.

ANGELA'S ANGER KEPT HER strong and focused as they drove into the mountains west of Denver. Neil's scheming had driven her to cancel her wedding moments before she was scheduled to say her vows. She was a runaway bride—the kind of low-class, ridiculous person who showed up on tawdry talk shows to jeer at the audience.

What kind of woman walked out on her own wedding?

She thought of the wilting floral decorations, the expensive invitations and the cake—Marie's spectacular five-tiered cake with alternating layers of lemon-vanilla and mocha-chocolate. Not to mention the gourmet menu for the reception dinner. All that food would go to waste. *How could I do this? I'm not this kind of person.*

She played by the rules, never cheated, tried to be kind and helpful. Everybody liked her, and she was glad for their approval. *Not anymore.* Imagining the faces of the wedding guests, she groaned inside. All those people must think the worst of her. Their sympathies would lie with Neil, of course. She'd be condemned as a heartless bitch who dumped her fiancé at the altar. Nobody would understand that she was the victim.

She corrected herself. *I'm not the victim. I escaped.* And she had absolutely nothing to feel guilty about. She'd rescued her son.

She glanced into the back, where Benjy had fallen asleep in his car seat. The late-afternoon sunlight warmed his face. His thick eyelashes formed perfect crescents on his cheeks. She would do anything and everything to protect him.

Her gaze swept from the backseat to the front and came to rest on Shane. They'd hardly spoken since they left the PRESS building. After he slipped a Johnny Cash CD into the dashboard player, he'd been talking on his hands-free phone, making arrangements. Now, he was as quiet as the surrounding forests that descended from jagged peaks to the edge of the winding two-lane road.

"I hope you know," she said, "that I trust you implicitly."

He nodded. "I get that a lot."

"I can't help noticing that we don't seem to be headed toward your house in Silver Plume."

"Because that's the first place Neil will look. Even that pea-brain Carlson would guess that location."

"Mind if I ask where we're going?"

"A little cabin that belongs to a guy I met a couple months ago. It's six miles down a dirt road into a canyon, the nearest neighbors are half a mile away and—here's the genius part—there's a high-tech alarm system."

"And your friend is okay with having us stay there?"

"I just talked to him. He's in California for the month doing some kind of consulting work for a software company. He's got some fancy computer equipment at the cabin. Benjy can probably figure out how it all works."

"Do you think these precautions are really necessary? Are we really in danger?"

"Yes."

She looked back at Benjy to make sure he was asleep and wouldn't overhear their conversation over the rumbling background music from Johnny Cash. "It's hard to imagine that Neil would threaten us. Not physically, anyway. He's a respected doctor."

"Who drugged you and arranged for a stalker and slashed your wedding gown."

Those were facts, indisputable. "How could I have been so wrong about him?"

"You're not to blame," Shane said. "Neil took a long time setting this trap. He laid the groundwork when you were still married to Tom."

And after Tom's death, Neil had really wanted her to have the IVF procedure. She remembered long, serious conversations with Neil holding her hand and telling her how much a baby would enrich her life. After Benjy was born, Neil had come to the hospital. He'd held the infant in his arms. "Maybe he thinks he has some kind of paternal connection to Benjy, that I never would have had the procedure if he hadn't encouraged me."

He shot her a stern glare. "You just can't help yourself, can you? You've got to see the best in everybody, even Neil."

"Am I that gullible?"

"You've got to take off the rose-colored glasses and see things the way they are. Neil is an arrogant son of a bitch who set out to hurt you and Benjy."

"You're right. I should forget about him and let it go. Getting married to Neil was a mistake that never happened."

"It won't be that easy," Shane warned. "There are too many unanswered questions."

She knew he was right. Neil wouldn't simply vanish into the night. Carlson had said it: Neil would never let her go. She had to be ready to stand up for herself. And for her son.

Chapter Thirteen

The first thing Angela did when they reached the cabin was to change into comfortable jeans and a T-shirt. She dashed into the bedroom and yanked off the suit. As she plucked the bobby pins from her hair, the super-hold hair spray she'd used to keep her up-do in place crackled and crunched. Too much in a hurry to look for a brush, she flipped her head upside down and dragged her fingers through the long strands until she had destroyed every trace of formality. She was free. Neil no longer controlled her life. No more pretending to enjoy dress-up receptions in borrowed jewels. Never again would she have to eat the swill prepared by his grumpy housekeeper.

Her lovely white wedding suit puddled on the hardwood floor. Her first impulse was to burn the damn thing, but she was far too practical to destroy an outfit she hadn't even worn once. She hung the suit in a closet that already held clothing belonging to Shane's friend.

While they stayed at the cabin, she and Benjy would be sharing the double bed in here. Since there was no other bedroom, Shane was stuck on the sofa.

With her long hair tumbling around her shoulders, she stepped into the open living room of the small cabin. To the right of the front door was a fireplace with the hide-a-bed sofa and two chairs that were homey but had definitely seen better days. The huge coffee table was a darker wood than the paneling on the walls. The kitchen screamed bachelor pad with a two-burner stove that was smaller than the microwave on the counter.

Shane's friend wouldn't win any housekeeping awards, but the cabin had a pleasantly rustic ambience—except for the office space to the left of the front door. An L-shaped desk held two computers and other high-tech equipment. The electronics didn't stop there. When they entered, Shane showed her how to deactivate the keypad alarm system, similar to the one he'd installed at her house.

While Shane put away the meager food supplies they'd picked up at a convenience store when he'd gassed up the Land Rover, Benjy charged toward her. He wrapped his arms around her legs and held on tight.

She scooped him up in her arms and kissed his pudgy cheeks. "How do you like the cabin?"

"Theodore Roosevelt did *not* live here."

"I don't suppose he did."

"There's no TV." His eyes strayed to the computer equipment. "Can I play with that?"

Now was as good a time as any to lay down some ground rules. The last thing she wanted was to ruin this valuable equipment. Inside the cabin, she ran through a list of things he could not touch without permission. Then, they stepped outside.

The log cabin perched on a wide ledge halfway up a steep road in a canyon. A log retaining wall kept the gravelly dirt from crumbling away beneath their feet. The covered porch stretched all the way across the front of the house. A hammock swung at one end, and there were two wooden rocking chairs.

Though many Colorado forests had been decimated by the pine beetles, the walls of this canyon above a trickling little creek were thick with Ponderosa pine and indigenous shrubs.

Benjy pointed at a chipmunk that scampered on the edge of the retaining wall. "Look."

Shane came onto the porch behind them. "Lots of critters live up here. Raccoons and skunks and squirrels. Plenty of deer and elk."

Benjy wiggled to get down. As soon as his toes touched the boards of the porch, he hopped down from the two-step stoop and ran toward the retaining wall where he'd seen the chipmunk.

"Be careful," she called after him.

There were dangers in the mountains. Her son could slip and tumble down the hillside. In addition to the friendly woodland creatures, she knew there were also bears and mountain lions. Even the plant life could be lethal. Though several species were edible, some of the brightest berries were poisonous.

As Benjy peered over the edge, she restrained herself from grabbing him and pulling him back. Though she would have liked to keep Benjy wrapped in a giant bubble of safety, she knew he had to explore and take risks.

"I have one rule," she said. "You don't go outside by yourself. One of us has to be with you."

"Okay, Mom."

The pristine front of his dress-up shirt was already smudged. "Let's go into the bedroom and get you into some better clothes for exploring."

He dashed for the door and she followed. Their rushed departure from her house meant that all Benjy's clothes had been flung into a black garbage bag. After a bit of digging, she found a long-sleeved T-shirt and a pair of jeans.

"You go now, Mommy. I can get dressed by myself."

She knew he could manage on his own, but she longed

for the days when he needed her to help him with snaps and buttons. Her little boy was growing up so fast.

As she left the room, she grabbed her shoulder bag. Then she joined Shane on the porch. "This place is terrific."

"The best part is that nobody knows about it. The guy who lives here keeps to himself. I'm probably the only visitor he's had since he moved up here."

Holding up her cell phone, she asked, "Can I turn it on?"

He warned, "There are ways of tracking the signal."

"But Neil is a doctor, not a superspy. Unless he hires somebody like PRESS to track me down, I don't think anybody will be triangulating my phone signal."

"You laid down the rules for Benjy," he said. "I'm going to do the same for you. No phone."

She clutched it to her breast. "Can I just check my messages?"

"Just this once. Then give it to me."

There were several calls from Neil which she skipped. She played back the message from Yvonne that was a simple, "You go, girl. Everything here is fine."

An unfamiliar number spiked her curiosity, and she played back the message. It was from Dr. Prentice.

"It's been a most unpleasant afternoon," he said solemnly, "filled with anger and speculation. I'm sure you believe you're doing the right thing, and I admire your fortitude. But I would very much like to talk. I might be able to give you some context for the present situation."

He suggested that they meet in person.

She turned off the phone and handed it to Shane. "Prentice wants to meet."

"Why?"

"He said something about giving context. Meeting him isn't a bad idea. He might have an explanation."

"Or he could be setting a trap."

Though she had no reason to suspect that Prentice had known about the plot to drive her crazy, the old doctor was clearly in Neil's camp. She couldn't trust him, but she desperately wanted answers. "I need to know why Neil did this. He didn't propose marriage because he loved me. That's for sure. But why? And why does he want custody of Benjy?"

"Tomorrow," Shane said. "We'll start investigating tomorrow."

She was anxious to get everything solved and neatly sorted out, but she trusted Shane. He'd been right about Neil. He was probably right about Prentice setting a trap.

Tomorrow would be soon enough.

THE NEXT DAY WAS TOO PERFECT. Angela had forgotten how much she loved being in the mountains. In the summer, the temperature was usually ten degrees cooler than in Denver. The air tasted fresh, and pure sunlight cleansed her senses. As she and Benjy strolled down the road to the creek running through the bottom of the canyon, the gravel crunched beneath her sneakers. She listened to the breeze as it ruffled the leaves of shrubs and whisked through pine needles. So peaceful. So beautiful. In the midst of all this natural beauty, she could almost forget that her life was in turmoil.

At the edge of the creek, Benjy got busy, throwing rocks into the cool, rippling water and poking into the dirt with a tangled stick. This was better than previous trips to the mountains; Benjy was the right age to enjoy the outdoors.

Her only complaint about the cabin was a lack of food supplies, and Shane had agreed. About an hour ago, he headed into town to shop. He'd told her to stay close to the cabin. If they heard a car coming, they should disappear.

Predictably, Benjy slipped on a rock and fell into the shallow creek. His whoops of laughter tickled her. Seeing him act like a regular kid gave her too much pleasure to scold him for not being careful. Kids were supposed to explore and get dirty.

As they climbed the road back to the cabin, Shane returned with the groceries. She'd given him a list of basics, but it was difficult to guess what they'd need. She didn't know whether they'd be staying here for a day or a week or a month.

He carried two huge cloth grocery bags into the kitchen and checked his wristwatch. "In eight minutes, I need to figure out how that computer works."

"Why eight minutes?"

"There's a satellite connection coming through."

"I'll help," Benjy said.

She took her son by the shoulders and pointed him toward the bedroom. "You need to change your clothes."

"Mom, I'm not cold."

"But you're wet. Go."

Grumbling, he dragged his feet as he left the room.

She stood behind Shane at the computer. "What's up?"

"I stopped by headquarters in the courthouse and did some research," he said as he followed a written list for various steps on the computer. "I wanted more information on how Prentice was involved in the murder of Dr. Raymond Jantzen."

She immediately remembered the study that dictated the circumstances of her birth. "Raymond Jantzen? Of the Prentice-Jantzen study?"

As he typed information into the computer, the screen

showed various menus. "I've set up a face-to-face talk with someone who was involved in the investigation. She was also one of the IVF babies in the study. Her name is Eve Weathers-Jantzen."

"Her name is Jantzen, too? What's her relationship to the man who was murdered?"

"Eve married Dr. Jantzen's son," Shane said. "He's stationed overseas, and she's accompanying him. Which is why you couldn't meet in person."

"Do we need the computer hookup? Can't you just tell me what she said?"

With a few more adjustments, he brought up a picture on the screen. The pixilated image showed a blue-eyed blonde woman wearing a green T-shirt that said, Geeks Rock.

Shane adjusted the audio. "Eve? Can you hear me?"

"Loud and clear. The satellite hookup is excellent."

Shane plunked her into the chair in front of the computer. "Eve, meet Angela Hawthorne."

Eve's mouth stretched in a gigantic smile, and she leaned forward as though she could come closer. "Wow, you're beautiful."

"Thank you." Angela returned the smile. "Where are you?"

"I could tell you, but I'd have to kill you." She laughed. "I've been waiting my whole life to say that. Sounds dramatic, doesn't it?"

Benjy rushed into the room. "I wanna see."

Angela popped him onto her lap and introduced him.

Though it didn't seem possible, Eve's smile got even wider. "Hey, Benjy."

"Do you know the thirteenth president?" he asked.

"Millard Fillmore," she said. "I always liked him because he ran for the Know Nothing Party."

Shane lifted Benjy off her lap. "We're going outside now. I saw some elk up on the ridge."

After they left, Eve said, "We don't have a lot of time on this connection. How much has Shane told you?"

"Nothing really. I know we were both part of the Prentice-Jantzen study, which means we're both twenty-six and born in New Mexico."

"And there are many more similarities." Eve's pixilated image on the screen cocked her head. "Would you mind pushing your hair back from your face?"

An odd request, but Angela complied.

"You have detached earlobes and a widow's peak. So do I." She ran her hands through her messy, shoulder-length blond hair. "These secondary genetic traits really don't prove much, but I have DNA analysis for every person involved in the study."

"Including me?"

"You and I were the only two females in a test field of twenty-four subjects. A statistical anomaly. There should have been more women, but the differential isn't necessarily outside the parameters of possibility. Since this study took place twenty-six years ago, I doubt that Dr. Prentice had the tools to manipulate the outcome."

Eve might look like a ditzy blonde, but her language showed a high level of education. "Are you a scientist?"

"Mathematician," she said. "And you?"

"I'm a chef."

"And I'll bet you're Cordon Bleu," Eve said. "Furthermore, I'd be willing to wager that you have exceptional comprehension skills. That's the plus side of Prentice's genetic engineering. We all have high IQs."

Neil had made a similar assumption, but Angela wasn't convinced. If she was so smart, why had she come within minutes of marrying a man who wanted to do her harm? "We should cut to the chase."

"Right," Eve said. "When Prentice set up his study, there were several sperm donors. Fewer women volunteered their eggs for harvesting. The in vitro process isn't a lot of fun."

"I've been through it," Angela said.

"Me, too."

Abruptly, the image on the screen shifted as Eve showed off her belly. "I'm five months' pregnant. Can you tell?"

Angela couldn't help grinning as she remembered her own excitement while she was carrying Benjy. "Bottom line, Eve."

Her face came back on the screen. "You and I have the same biological mother. We're half sisters."

Chapter Fourteen

Her sister? Angela felt her jaw drop. This couldn't be. *My sister?* Those two words—words that other people took for granted—were as incomprehensible to her as a foreign language.

She'd never felt as if she was part of a real family. When her father died, she was too young to remember him. There were photographs and a stuffed bunny rabbit that he supposedly bought for her. But the warm place in her memory where her father should have been was a blank.

Her mother had tried to make a life for them, but she hadn't signed up to be a single mother, and Angela knew that dragging a child from place to place was a burden. She'd tried to be a good girl, tried to make herself useful. But her mom seldom smiled.

After she got married again, Mom cheered up. At least, she wasn't crying herself to sleep every night, and Angela was glad for that, even though she felt like an outsider in her stepfamily.

"I don't have any living relatives except for Benjy." She drew back from the smiling blonde woman on the computer screen. "My mother died when I was eighteen."

"I'm sorry," Eve said gently. "It must be tough."

"I do all right." Self-reliance was a huge part of her character. There hadn't been a choice.

"The people who raised you, the people you called Mom and Dad, aren't your biological parents."

"I understand." Dr. Prentice had explained that part of the study.

"Then you know I'm not lying. Biologically, I'm your half sister," Eve said with absolute assurance. "That makes Benjy my nephew. And my baby will be his cousin."

Angela's doubts faded as she imagined the Thanksgiving dinners they could share, the homemade birthday presents she could fashion and the special dinners she could prepare. "What's your favorite food?"

"I'm developing a taste for hummus."

"I have a perfect recipe." But now probably wasn't the time to talk about food. "I want to meet you."

"As soon as I'm back in Denver," Eve promised. "In the meantime, Shane tells me that you've got a problem."

"The worst part is already over. I called off the wedding."

"Do you think your former fiancé is going to accept your decision and let you go?"

"Doubtful. And that's not because he loves me and can't live without me."

"Did you love him?" Eve asked.

"I must have. I agreed to marry him, but we didn't have a grand passion." She could have been talking to Yvonne or any of her other friends, but this conversation was different because Eve was her sister. Every word echoed with a deeper understanding. "We hadn't made love in weeks. Maybe a month."

"That sucks."

"Not too much. I've never been all that thrilled about what goes on in the bedroom. Not even with my first husband, and I definitely loved him." She couldn't believe she'd confided such a personal, intimate detail. "I've never told anyone that before."

"I'm no expert on sex," Eve said. "Until I met Blake, I was a virgin. But believe me, when it's done right, there's nothing better than sexual intercourse. And foreplay, of course. Lots of kissing and touching and—"

Her image on the screen was interrupted by static, reminding Angela that this satellite connection wouldn't last forever. She needed to focus. "Here's my problem. My ex-fiancé wants custody of my son. But I don't know why."

"If Prentice is involved, there's some kind of genetic connection. Do you have a DNA profile for Benjy?"

"I don't need one. After my husband was killed, I had the IVF procedure using a frozen embryo. My son's DNA is mine and my husband's."

Or was it? Her mind raced as she imagined alternate scenarios. She and Tom had gone to Dr. Prentice; they had trusted him. What if he had substituted a different embryo? She might be another unwitting participant in a genetic engineering experiment. Like her mother.

"All the same," Eve said, "run a check on Benjy's DNA. And anybody else you can think of. Your ex-fiancé. His family."

An impossible idea! "I can't ask them for DNA swabs."

The image jumped on the screen as Eve gestured emphatically. "Science might be the only way to get direct answers. Prentice likes to play God. Don't trust anything he says."

"Was he responsible for the murder of…" she paused for a moment while she thought of the proper relationship "…your father-in-law?"

"No," Eve said. "As far as I know, Prentice isn't a murderer. Just a scumbag."

"Do you think I should meet with him?"

"You might get answers, but I don't know if you want to get that close to him. Talk to Shane about it." Eve's wide mouth stretched in a toothy grin. "By the way, what's your relationship with him?"

"Shane is my best friend."

"Can I offer you some advice? Sisterly advice?"

Angela couldn't help smiling back at the image on the screen. "Can I stop you?"

"Probably not. Once I get started, I obsess on a subject until it's completely exhausted. Okay, here's my advice. Hang on to Shane. He's a good guy."

"Very good advice."

"I've got to go. We'll stay in touch via e-mail. And I'll send a copy of your DNA profile."

Angela reached out and touched the screen. "I always wanted a sister."

"Me, too." Eve was also touching the screen. "Give my nephew a big hug."

Static raced across the screen, and the picture dissolved.

For a moment, Angela sat back in the chair, trying to absorb what had just happened. Then she rushed for the door. She couldn't wait to tell Shane about her new family relationship.

Outside, he leaned against the porch railing, watching as Benjy scampered back and forth, gathering pinecones. Shane turned to look at her, tilted his cowboy hat back on his forehead and raised an eyebrow. "What's up? You look like you stuck your finger in a light socket."

"I have a sister." Though she wanted to shout the news, she whispered so Benjy wouldn't hear. "Half sister, actually. We have the same biological mother."

"You and Eve don't look much alike."

"Apparently, we share secondary genetic traits." She heard herself repeating Eve's language. "Whatever that means."

Her gaze settled on her son as he scurried toward her with two fistfuls of pinecones. When he got to the porch stoop, he hopped from one foot to the other. With each hop, he recited a U.S. president's name in a singsong cadence.

In a quiet voice, she asked Shane, "Should I tell him about his new aunt?"

"That's up to you."

Angela was certain that Eve and Benjy would love each other. Their coloring was similar—blondish hair and blue eyes, though Benjy's eyes were an unusual color of dark, stormy blue. Still, the genetic connection between Eve and Benjy was obvious in their intelligence. When it came to genius behavior, her son counted as a brilliant example of genetic engineering. *What if he isn't my biological child?*

If Prentice had created her son using some kind of superembryo, she could understand why Neil wanted custody so badly. Neil must have been watching Benjy grow, waiting until his intelligence could be confirmed.

She turned toward Shane. "I need to set up a meeting with Prentice."

THAT NIGHT AFTER BENJY was tucked into bed, Shane opened a bottle of merlot and poured a healthy dose into two mismatched water glasses. In the front room, he delivered one glass to Angela, who sat on the plaid sofa with her feet curled up underneath her. She smiled up at him. Her long hair curled around her cheeks and spilled down her back. Ever since she'd talked to her half sister, her mood had fluctuated between bubbly happiness and flatout worry.

He sank into the chair beside the sofa, stretched out his legs, took a sip of wine and waited for her to confide in him.

"Nice wine," she said. "Can you do a DNA profile on Benjy?"

"Sure."

"How does it work?"

"I swab his cheek, seal it in a plastic bag and turn it in at the sheriff's office in Georgetown."

"How long will it take to get results?"

"If I mark it urgent, it ought to take only a couple of weeks."

She groaned. "That long? On TV, they get results in a couple of minutes."

"We don't exactly have a high-tech crime lab in Clear Creek County." Most of the local crime involved bar fights, domestic violence and vehicular issues. There were, however, exceptions. Two years ago, he'd investigated a rape case and wanted DNA results from semen in a hurry so he could put the offender behind bars. "I know somebody who can rush the results. It'll be only a couple of days."

"Eve suggested that I test Benjy. She said that if Prentice is involved, DNA is an issue."

The implication was clear. "She thinks Prentice might have substituted a different embryo for your in vitro procedure."

"Because of the Prentice-Jantzen study, I wasn't the biological child of my parents." Her eyebrows pulled into a scowl that caused parallel worry lines. "It's possible that Benjy isn't mine."

That suspicion had been dancing at the edge of his mind since he heard about Prentice's fraud in the study, but he hadn't voiced it. Angela had enough to worry about without second-guessing her child's biological heritage.

He drew up his legs, leaned forward in the chair and placed his glass of wine on the coffee table. His arms were open to comfort her and hold her. "Benjy will always be your son. His DNA doesn't matter."

She rubbed at her forehead to erase the worry lines. "When I first decided to have the IVF procedure, I wanted Tom's child. By having his baby, I thought I could keep a piece of him with me forever."

"I remember."

Tom's death had left her devastated. Even when she smiled, her eyes were a deep well of sorrow. A shadow of that sadness veiled her face.

"Sometimes," she said, "I still miss him."

"So do I."

"I'll always be his widow. I have my precious memories of Tom and of our time together. But I have my own life—the life I've built with Benjy. And with Waffles. Even with Neil." She gave an ironic laugh. "In a way, I should be grateful to him for helping me make a transition. By accepting his proposal, I realized that I could be married to another man."

"As long as it's the right man."

Her eyes brightened as she gazed at him over the rim of her glass. "Are you saying I should look for someone who's not trying to drive me insane?"

"Whatever floats your boat."

The stillness of the mountains wrapped comfortably around them. On quiet nights like this, he almost regretted his decision to move into town and work for Josh at PRESS. But that was because Angela was here. Her presence turned the solitude into peace. If he'd been alone in this cabin, he'd be itching to roam.

She shifted position on the sofa. "Eve also said I should

try to get DNA from everybody involved. Do you think there's any way to track down Neil's genetic profile?"

"I doubt that he's in the CODIS data bank of criminal DNA. I know the military has a lot of DNA records on file."

"Neil was never in the military, but his father was. Can we access that information?"

"Doubtful." An idea occurred to him. "What about Neil's mother? Nobody ever talks about her. She might be willing to provide a DNA sample."

"I don't know how to reach her."

Mentally, Shane put that research on his list of things to do: find Neil's mother. At this point, his to-do list was very short. Apart from keeping Angela and Benjy away from Neil, he didn't have a plan. "We need to come up with some kind of strategy."

"Starting with Prentice," she said. "Neil isn't going to stop coming after me until he knows for sure that there isn't a chance for him to get his hands on Benjy. I can negotiate, starting with Prentice."

"In a phone call."

"In person," she said firmly. "I want him to know I'm serious. To look him in the eye."

"Could be dangerous."

"Not if we meet in a public place. What's he going to do? Shoot me?"

The thought of Angela seeing anybody associated with Neil worried him. Whether or not she wanted to believe it, she was vulnerable. "I can set it up, and I'll make sure there's no chance for Neil to get anywhere near you."

"I need to find answers," she said. "After I talked to Eve, I started wondering when this plot to get custody of Benjy started. Prentice told me that he discovered I was part of the study when he ran my DNA for the embryo process."

"But he might have known earlier."

Prentice might have been targeting her all along. His lecture, which had so impressed Tom, might have been a setup. Neil might have been in on it from the start. "Do you remember what Dr. Em said? Neil purposely went after you when he saw you at the Army Medical Center. What if his good friend Dr. Prentice told him that you were special?"

"I was also married," she said. "Happily married."

Shane didn't think a woman's marital status would stop somebody like Neil—a guy with an ego as big as Mount Evans. "He might have thought he could steal you away."

"No way." She shook her head. "Neil and Tom met at the Army Medical Center. They weren't buddies or anything, but I remember that they talked about all the horrible diseases. The bird flu. And anthrax. And malaria. All of which might affect future children."

"Neil's conversation backed up Prentice's lecture." A sinister picture began to take shape in his mind. "They were working in tandem, warning him about exposures that could cause sterility or genetic problems for your kids."

If their plan had been to convince Tom that the only rational course was to create frozen embryos, it had worked. Tom had been adamant. He couldn't wait to get to Prentice and start the process.

"But why?" she asked.

"You said it yourself. You were biologically engineered. You have genius DNA."

"So what? What did Prentice hope to gain?"

"Your eggs."

Her eyes widened. "Okay, it sounds weird when you say that out loud."

But he was thinking darker thoughts. Prentice had needed Tom to convince her to undergo the process for creating their frozen embryos. Once her eggs had been harvested, there was no longer a need for her husband.

Tom's death in an unsolved hit-and-run accident seemed far too convenient.

Chapter Fifteen

The next morning, Angela went for a jog on the gravel road outside the cabin. First, she ran downhill toward the creek where the rushing water slipped like satin over the rocks, then she took a turn that went higher and higher. Jogging in mountain terrain was more of a cardio workout than she was accustomed to, and when she reached the top of the ridge, she stopped to catch her breath. On one side, the two-lane graded road dropped away, revealing a spectacular panorama of rugged foothills and jagged peaks. Hands on hips, she walked.

Physically, she felt better than she had in weeks. Maybe months. Her body had recovered from whatever was in those nasty blue pills Neil prescribed. Whenever she thought of what a chump she'd been, her anger exploded like a pressure cooker.

Neil had been clever. She had to give him points for sneakiness. She hadn't suspected his treachery until Shane opened her eyes. Now, her vision was 20/20, and she had to say that her future *without Neil* looked pretty good.

As soon as this was over, she'd go back to her regular life, taking care of Benjy and running Waffles. One of her regular patrons at the restaurant had been encouraging her to put together a book of her breakfast recipes. Maybe she'd take on that challenge.

And Shane would be living in Denver, working at PRESS. She hoped he'd stay at her house while he got settled. Having him around was no bother. The opposite, in fact. She'd enjoy making him dinner every night, going for walks in the evening, taking Benjy to the zoo on weekends. Maybe he'd stay with them for a long time.

She started jogging again.

In just a few hours, she was scheduled to meet with Prentice at a roadside café outside Silver Plume. Shane had laid out the strategy for this meeting with the foresight of a general.

The first thing to do was to drop off Benjy so he'd be safe. While she was meeting with Prentice, her son would be staying at a local horse ranch. The owner was a friend of Shane's family, and there would be other kids for Benjy to play with.

When they got to the café, Shane wouldn't accompany her inside. He had already arranged with the café owner to have her seated at a booth next to the front window where he could watch from the parking lot and be ready to intervene if Prentice tried anything.

As she jogged the last few yards to the cabin, her legs felt springy and strong. With any luck, she could get the answers she wanted from Prentice and negotiate an end to her unfortunate association with Neil Revere.

WHEN ANGELA DROVE Shane's Land Rover into the parking lot outside the Grizzly Bear Café, she understood why Shane had chosen this meeting place. The café sat at the far end of a wide clearing beside the road with nothing else around; it would be nearly impossible to stage an ambush here. Cars and trucks parked across the front and on either side of the large asphalt lot.

The restaurant was a dark wood structure about the

length of two trailers laid end to end. Above the entrance that bisected the front of the building was a faded picture of a grizzly, showing his claws. Windows stretched across either side. Though she knew Shane was already here, she didn't spot him in the parking lot.

Anticipation raised her pulse rate. She was excited to face Prentice and learn what was behind Neil's scheme.

When she entered and introduced herself to the man behind the cash register, he gave her a wink and escorted her to the window booth. After a quick glance at the menu, she ordered an orange soda and a buffalo burger. Not that she was hungry. But as a restaurant owner, she felt obliged to place an order if she was taking up space in a booth.

Before her food arrived, Dr. Prentice marched through the entrance as though he owned the place. Though his clinic was in the mountains, the exclusive Aspen lifestyle was a long way from Grizzly Bear Café. His jeans were tailored, and his fawn-colored leather vest had never been dirtied by an honest day's work.

He sat across from her with his shoulders straight and his chin tilted back. Adjusting his thick glasses, he looked down his long nose with an attitude of disdain. She remembered what Eve had said: this man liked to play God.

"Good afternoon, Angela."

His voice grated on her nerves. "Good afternoon."

"I must say, you surprised all of us when you called off the wedding. Many of the guests had already arrived, and there was no time to contact the others. We had to tell them all that you had a change of heart." A cruel smile touched his lips. "Some of them thought you were having a nervous breakdown."

Which was exactly what Neil wanted them to think. Had she unwittingly played into his hands? "I don't care what they thought."

"All those gifts will have to be returned."

"Neil should have considered the inconvenience before he drugged me."

"He was only trying to help you get over your insomnia. Is it possible that you overreacted?"

"Hardly." Though he ticked her off, she held her anger in check. "An overreaction would have been if I'd gone after Neil with a cleaver."

He signaled to the waitress. "I'd like a bottled water."

"I've spoken to Eve," she said.

His thick gray eyebrows rose above the rim of his glasses. "I thought she and her husband were out of the country."

"We talked via computer. She told me about the Prentice-Jantzen study. We're half sisters. Is that correct?"

"Yes, it is."

"Do I have any other genetic siblings?"

"I can't say. My part in the study didn't involve checking the DNA profiles for other matches. All I did was create twenty-four embryos from superior subjects. Many—like Eve—have established successful careers in complex, professional fields."

In spite of herself, she was curious. "And the others?"

"Those like yourself," he said. "You mustn't feel that your accomplishments are lesser than those of scientists or doctors, Angela. You're a creative person."

The way he said *creative* made it sound like something disgusting. "Are there other chefs?"

"There are musicians and an artist. All are high achievers, despite the fact that they were raised by average individuals. That was my thesis. Genetics trumps environment."

Though she could have argued the point, she hadn't arranged this meeting to discuss his crackpot theories. "When, exactly, did you know that I was one of your subjects?"

"As I told you, when you and your husband came to me."

That coincidence was just too handy to be believed. The odds against having her—out of all the people in the world—come to him must be astronomical. Eve, the mathematician, could probably give her a number.

Angela took a poke at his arrogance. "You must have felt like a complete fool when I showed up. There were only twenty-four subjects in the study. How could you lose track of me?"

He shrugged. "After your father died, your mother was in Europe. She didn't respond to any of our queries. After she remarried, she changed both of your names."

"All a matter of public record," Angela said. "We weren't in the witness protection program or anything. The Army was always able to keep track of her."

"For the purposes of our study, we needed consistent annual updates, which ceased when your father passed away. You were dropped from the list when you failed to comply."

"I was four years old."

"The failure," he said, "was your mother's."

Under the table, her hands drew into fists. Her mom wasn't the best parent in the world, but she didn't deserve to be called a failure. Angela swallowed the aggressive response that rose to her lips.

Talking to Prentice wasn't about getting even. She needed information. "Nevertheless," she said, "if you had wanted to find me, you could have done so."

"It's possible."

"Even after you supposedly figured out who I was, you avoided telling me the truth."

"It wasn't relevant."

The waitress arrived with his bottled water and her

buffalo burger with golden, crispy fries. Her gut clenched so tightly that she doubted she could stuff food down her throat.

But she lifted the burger and took a bite as if to prove that she wasn't rattled. She picked up a French fry and studied it with the kind of attention reserved for rare white truffles. She pointed the fry toward him. "Want a taste?"

Disregarding her offer, he sipped his water. "We need to talk about Neil. And I want to make this perfectly clear."

"Oh, please do," she said. "And speak in words of one syllable so I can understand."

"There's no need for sarcasm."

"Blame it on my creative side."

"Neil knew nothing about the stalking. It was all Carlson's idea. When Neil asked him to keep an eye on you, he got carried away."

She didn't buy one word of this explanation. "I wouldn't have thought Carlson was so clever."

"He has an unfortunate immaturity, but he's actually very bright. I referred him to Neil."

She filed that bit of information away for future reference. "Is Carlson from Aspen?"

"I met him there. At the time, he was a ski bum who dropped out of med school. You must believe me when I say that Carlson is terribly sorry for upsetting you."

Yeah, sure. "He sounded real apologetic when he was yelling at me in a parking lot outside the PRESS office."

"And, of course, Neil is devastated."

A twinge of guilt went through her, but she quickly banished any thought of sympathy. "He'll get over it."

"You and Neil are very well suited for each other. A good genetic match. You'd have remarkable offspring."

"Like Benjy?"

At the mention of her son's name, his cold attitude

thawed, and his smile turned sincere. Prentice morphed into the kindly grandfather she'd seen when they met at Neil's house. "Benjy is an exceptional child. So many people claim their children are gifted. So few truly are."

She hesitated before asking the question she desperately wanted answered: *Is Benjy mine?* No way would he give her an honest reply. He'd been content to deceive the twenty-four childless couples in the Prentice-Jantzen study.

Instead, she came at the issue from a different angle. "I'm having Benjy tested. I should have his DNA profile in just a few days."

The mask of kindness fell from his face. "Before you do anything rash, I want you to meet with Neil."

"I have nothing to say to him. I won't change my mind."

"It would be so simple. I have a cabin not far from here. I could take you there now."

She was immediately suspicious. "Is Neil at your cabin? Is he nearby?"

"Come with me," Prentice urged. "Just for an hour. Neil deserves that much. You humiliated him by calling off the wedding."

"I'm not the villain. Neil was trying to drive me insane. Did he tell you about slashing my wedding gown to shreds? Did he mention the hidden microphones designed to wake me each night at the moment when Tom died?"

"As I explained, Carlson was responsible for—"

"Carlson had nothing to do with that vile pre-nup," she said. "Carlson wasn't responsible for the carefully worded section in that document that gave Neil custody of my son. Why is he trying to take Benjy away from me?"

As soon as she blurted out those words, she knew she'd made a mistake. Her goal had been to cleverly trick Prentice into revealing some deeper truth, but she'd thrown her cards on the table and shown her hand. She'd let him see her greatest fear.

"You're being absurd," Prentice said.

"Am I? Isn't it true that Neil was only marrying me to get to my son?"

"My dear, I never realized you were so high-strung. You remind me of Neil's mother. Even at her best, she was a very high-maintenance woman."

She refused to let him sidestep the custody issue by changing the subject. "Answer my question, Doctor. Was Neil marrying me to gain access to Benjy?"

"I'm simply trying to help you understand—to gain a full picture. You can keep an open mind, can't you?"

"Not when it comes to my son."

"Such determination might be admirable if it weren't so misplaced. You need to know about Neil's mother."

"Why?"

"I'm not a psychologist, but my dear friend Ray Jantzen would say that men often choose wives who remind them of their mothers." He shrugged. "In this instance, the comparison could be significant. You see, Neil's mother has been hospitalized for years. She's a delusional schizophrenic. Tragic, really."

Was he accusing her of being psychotic? She sputtered, unable to find the words to respond to such an over-the-top allegation.

"Think about it," he said. "Neil's concern about your mental health—as evidenced in the pre-nup—could possibly derive from memories of his mother and what he went through with her."

She grabbed her shoulder bag and fished out her wallet to pay for the uneaten buffalo burger. "This conversation is over."

"Angela, Angela." He took off his glasses and rubbed the bridge of his nose. "Why won't you listen to reason?"

She took out a twenty—which provided a more than ample tip—and placed it on the table as she scooted out of the booth. "Don't contact me again. I'm done with Neil and with you."

Before she could run out the door, he grabbed her wrist. "You won't get rid of me that easily."

Anger surged through her veins. She glared into his face. Then, she gasped.

His eyes! Without his glasses, she could clearly see his eyes. They were the same unusual blue-gray as Benjy's.

Chapter Sixteen

Technically, Shane was on duty today. He'd given his two weeks' notice but was still a Park County deputy sheriff. In spite of his navy-blue uniform shirt and his badge, his heart wasn't in his work. He'd ignored two calls from the dispatcher regarding a speeder in nearby Georgetown. It went against his grain to do a half-assed job, but today the other deputies would have to pick up the slack. His only focus was on keeping Angela safe.

In the parking lot outside the Grizzly Bear Café, he'd changed positions several times, making certain that no one—neither Carlson nor Neil—was lurking in the nearby trees. He leaned against the side of the patrol vehicle where he had an unobstructed view through the front window of the restaurant. Even from a distance, he could tell that Angela was plenty angry.

On his walkie-talkie, he communicated with the other deputy he'd posted at the rear of the restaurant. "You see anything?"

"All clear. How much longer do we have to stay?"

Through the window, he saw Angela stand up. "Only a couple of minutes. It looks like she's leaving."

He kept his eye on Prentice as Angela headed toward the exit. The old man was using his cell phone, probably reporting back to Neil. Shane glanced toward the far edge of the lot where Prentice had parked his vehicle—a Cadillac Escalade SUV that he'd angled across two spaces to keep anyone from bumping the chrome.

When Angela emerged from the restaurant, Shane got into the patrol vehicle. Their plan was for her to drive a safe distance away from the café before they met up. Her high ponytail bounced as she stormed toward his Land Rover with car keys in hand. Her shoulders were tense. She looked as mad as the grizzly on the sign over the café entrance.

He spoke into the walkie-talkie. "We're done here. Come around front, and I'll buy you lunch."

"You owe me more than that, buddy. I want a full breakfast cooked by Angela with crepes and that egg thing she does."

"Frittata," he said with a grin. "You got it."

Two years ago, Angela and baby Benjy had visited him for a week. Though she was supposed to be relaxing, she'd put together a breakfast for everybody at the courthouse. Some of the deputies were still talking about the frittatas, and at least four of them had asked her to marry them after tasting her cooking. He leaned forward to slip his key into the ignition.

He heard the squeal of tires, looked up and saw a black sedan swerve into the parking lot. The driver's-side door flew open. Neil jumped out.

"Son of a bitch," Shane muttered. He exited his vehicle and crossed the parking lot at a run. The adrenaline was already coursing through his veins. His hand was already on the gun at his hip.

Standing only a few feet away from Neil, Angela held up her hand. "Shane, stop. It's okay."

Not in his opinion. He didn't want Neil anywhere near her. She might think of this guy as a respected doctor, but

Shane saw a dangerous man who was accustomed to getting everything he wanted. "Show me your hands, Neil."

"Are you kidding?"

"That's an order," Shane barked.

Neil looked him up and down, taking in the obvious fact that Shane was an armed lawman. He raised both hands and turned in a circle. "Satisfied?"

"Not really." He'd like to arrest Neil for reckless driving, causing a public nuisance and being a general pain in the butt.

"Really," Angela said. "I can handle this."

"You've got five minutes."

"Would you mind stepping back?" Neil asked. "We'd like some privacy."

"Matter of fact," Shane drawled, "I do mind."

He stayed exactly where he was—about four feet away from them. His weight balanced on the balls of his feet, and his arms hung loose at his sides. At the slightest provocation, he would react with a vengeance.

Neil turned toward Angela. "I had hoped that you'd listen to reason and come along with Dr. Prentice."

"I'm actually glad you showed up," she said. "I gave Prentice a very clear message, but it's good to tell you in person so you can see my face and know that I'm serious."

"I'm listening," he said.

"Stay away from my son."

"That's not fair. I'd be a good father to Benjy. You know that. You know that I can give him everything he needs to develop into an extraordinary individual. He'd have the best tutors. He'd attend schools for gifted children."

"I know what my son needs."

"What?" He scoffed. "Peanut butter and jelly pancakes?"

"It's the same thing every child needs. The love of his parents."

Neil seemed taken aback. The muscle in his jaw worked as he tried to think of what to say next. In a tone of barely suppressed fury, he said, "You know I love Benjy."

"Not exactly," she said. "You value his intelligence. You want to show him off, to have him recite all the presidents like a trained monkey. He's more than a brain, more than potential. He's a little boy who needs to run around and get dirty and throw pebbles in a creek."

"Oh, I see. And I suppose you consider it a vital use of his time to hang around in a cheap breakfast restaurant."

"That's my decision. I'm his mother."

"Angela, please. I don't want to hurt you. We can work out our problems. For Benjy's sake."

She shook her head. "There's nothing to work out."

"I'm willing to forgive you."

Shane heard a note of desperation in Neil's voice—a sure indication that he was near the breaking point and, therefore, more of a threat. Shane cleared his throat as a reminder that he was still nearby. "Neil, it's time for you to move on."

"We don't need your interference." He wheeled around to face Shane. "You've done enough, poisoning her mind against me. Everything was fine until you came along."

"Fine?" Angela snapped. "Is it just fine for you to drug me? To have your little protégé stalk me?"

He swung back to face her. "Come back to me, Angela. We can still be married. There doesn't have to be a big ceremony. All we need is a justice of the peace."

She stuck out her chin. "Go to hell."

"You little bitch." He grabbed hold of her shoulders. "You can't say no to me. I won't let you."

Shane caught hold of his left arm, intending to separate

him from Angela. As he yanked them apart, Neil's right hand flicked out. If he hadn't been off balance, he would have slapped her face. As it was, he hit her shoulder. The force of his blow was enough to knock her backward into the car.

Shane twisted Neil's left arm behind his back and shoved hard. Neil stumbled and toppled forward. His knees collapsed. In seconds, he was lying facedown in the parking lot. Shane cuffed him.

He looked toward Angela. "Are you all right?"

Mutely, she nodded. She held her shoulder where Neil had made contact. Her eyes were wide and surprised as though she couldn't believe what had just taken place.

The other deputy joined them, and Shane left Neil to him as he went to Angela. "Are you sure you're not hurt?"

"I'm fine."

"I want you to take my car and follow us to the courthouse. We need to get you a restraining order." He checked her for symptoms of shock. Her breathing was regular and steady. Her pupils weren't dilated. "Are you okay to drive?"

"Totally fine," she repeated in a firm voice. She leaned closer to him and whispered, "You saved me again, my hero."

While she got in the car, Shane and the other deputy hauled Neil to his feet. With great satisfaction, Shane said, "Neil Revere, you're under arrest for assault."

"You won't get away with this," Neil snarled.

Shane dug into Neil's pocket for his car keys which he handed to the other deputy. "Would you mind moving the car? It's blocking the parking lot."

"No problem."

He escorted Neil to the police vehicle and stood facing

him. "Here's the deal. Angela is going to take out a restraining order. You can't come within a hundred feet of her."

"Do you think you can stop me?"

"A word of advice. Don't push me."

"What are you going to do?"

Constrained by his duty as a deputy, Shane fought the urge to drive his fist into Neil's gut. Beating a man in handcuffs wasn't his style, but he might be willing to make an exception for Neil.

"Someday," he said, "you and I are going to meet face-to-face, man-to-man. And I'll teach you what happens when you threaten women and children."

"You can't hurt me. I'll be out on bail within a few hours."

"Not until after you've gone through the booking process. You know the drill. The photograph. The fingerprinting. And the DNA swab."

"A DNA swab?"

"Standard procedure," Shane said, even though they seldom bothered with DNA. "Then you'll be locked in a holding cell along with the other local miscreants."

None too gently, he shoved his prisoner into the back of the car.

He glanced toward the far end of the parking lot. Prentice's fancy SUV was gone. A clean getaway.

SHANE WOULD BE WILLING to wager a month's salary that the arrest and booking process was unlike anything Neil Revere had ever experienced. Since everybody at the courthouse knew he'd attacked Angela and she happened to be their number one favorite chef, the officers treated him with as much disrespect as the law allowed. Their timing was such that Neil was assured of spending the night in a jail cell. Shane wished the accommodations had been more medieval—like a dungeon.

After Angela had filed her restraining order, they headed out toward the horse ranch where Benjy had been spending the afternoon. Their route navigated a maze of side roads to get there. Shane had chosen this place because it was off the beaten path.

While he drove, Angela filled him in on her meeting with Prentice. She mentioned that Prentice owned property in this general area and that Carlson had lived in Aspen at one time. Both of these leads would help in getting to the bottom of Neil's motives and the scheme he had intended to carry out.

"Anything else?" he asked.

Her shoulder twitched as though she wanted to dodge the question. "I don't think so."

Her high ponytail was unfastened and her hair tumbled around her face, shielding her expression, but she couldn't hide her feelings. Not only was she a lousy liar but he knew her well enough to sense her moods and her attitudes.

"You might as well tell me," he said.

"Tell you what?"

"You're holding something back. And it's going to eat at you until you finally blurt it out." He knew how her mind worked. "The more information I have, the sooner we get to the bottom of this."

"His eyes," she said. "Prentice took off his glasses and I saw the color of his eyes. Blue-gray. Exactly the same color as Benjy's."

It took a moment for him to absorb the weight of her observation. Prentice was involved in genetic engineering and had created the frozen embryo used in Angela's IVF procedure. Could he have used his own sperm? "We need to talk to Eve again. She might know where we can access Prentice's DNA profile."

"What if he's Benjy's biological father?" The twin worry lines between her brows appeared as her eyes narrowed. "I know it shouldn't bother me. I know that Benjy is my son no matter what the genetics. But damn!"

"We'll figure it out. I promise we'll find the truth."

"Maybe it's better if I don't know," she said.

Eve and her husband had come to the same conclusion. After they'd learned that all the babies in the Prentice-Jantzen study were not the biological offspring of the parents who raised them, they decided against making that information public.

Shane didn't agree. He would have arrested Prentice for fraud and informed the injured parties. At least Eve and her husband had insisted that Prentice close down his practice in Aspen and retire so he couldn't cause further harm.

Shane turned onto a two-lane gravel road. They were only a few miles from the horse ranch. "Prentice should have to pay for his crime. He experimented without your permission, violated your trust."

"Violated," she said. "That's a good word for how I feel."

"When Benjy's DNA test comes back—"

"I won't prosecute," she said. "I don't want to go through a trial. Prentice is a well-connected man who can hire good lawyers. I'm sure this case would be tied up in court for years, and the process would be more hurtful for me than for him. No way. As long as Prentice can't hurt anybody else, I don't care what he does."

Her reaction reminded him of a rape victim refusing to testify. Angela hadn't been assaulted, but the result was the same. Gently, he said, "This isn't your fault."

"Pull over," she said. "I need to take a minute to calm

down before I see Benjy. He's a smart little guy. As soon as he sees me, he'll know I'm upset."

He parked. On one side of the road was a forested hillside. The other was fenced.

Angela left the car and went toward the trees. Without a word, she hiked up the sloping hill, picking her way through pines and shrubs. She moved at a quick pace for a flatlander who wasn't acclimated to the altitude, but that didn't surprise him. She'd always been an avid runner.

They were almost out of sight of his vehicle when she turned and faced him. Her cheeks flushed red. Her breasts rose and fell as she sucked down one deep breath after another.

He couldn't tell if she was going to burst into tears or scream or let go with a string of curses. Whatever her response, he was here for her.

"If it weren't for you," she said, "I'd be falling apart right now."

"Give yourself some credit." He stepped up beside her. "You're plenty strong enough to stand on your own two feet."

She went up on tiptoe to kiss his cheek. At the last minute, she changed directions. Her soft, full lips pressed against his.

In that moment, everything changed.

Chapter Seventeen

Angela hadn't meant to kiss Shane, hadn't meant to touch him, hadn't meant to feel this burst of attraction. He was her best friend, someone she could trust, someone she cared for deeply. She loved him. *But not this way.*

Intending to apologize for overstepping an unspoken boundary, she tilted her head back and looked up. The boughs of the tall pines formed a ladder reaching into the skies. But all she saw was the blue of his eyes, and in them her desire reflected.

Deliberately, she glided her hand up his chest and around his neck. She pulled him close and kissed him for real. Her lips parted, and she drew his breath into her mouth.

He didn't move. His body was like granite, strong and steady. Even if she'd had a momentary lapse of judgment, he would resist.

She stammered, "I…I'm sorry."

"I'm not."

His hand clasped her waist, and he molded her body against his. They fit perfectly, as though they were meant to be joined. He kissed her back.

There was nothing gentle about the way his mouth worked over hers. Nothing timid about his hard, muscular body. Nothing reserved about the pure masculine energy sweeping over her.

In his arms, her heart was singing. A strange and wonderful heat coursed through her veins. He lifted her off the ground, and her legs wrapped around him. She clenched her thighs and held on, never wanting to let go.

Her back was against the trunk of a tree. They twined together so tightly that it seemed as if they were part of the forest. They had grown together.

Coming up for air, she inhaled a sharp gasp. A first kiss was supposed to be clumsy and hesitant, but Shane was masterful in his passion. His gaze penetrated deep inside her.

"I've waited so long," he murmured.

"Me, too." And here he was—a man she already loved as a friend. A lover? "I didn't know, didn't even know that I was waiting. Did you? Did you know?"

"In my dreams."

He eased his grasp and her legs slipped free. Her toes touched the ground. "You dreamed about me?"

"Being with you was more than I could hope for."

She tasted his mouth again. His kiss was magic, sparking tremors and shivers that she'd never experienced before. Her entire body—from the roots of her hair to her toenails—seemed to shimmer. "I don't want to stop."

"We don't have to."

But she knew better. Not matter how much she wanted to tear off his clothes and make love right here and now, she was a responsible person. They both were. "We're already late to pick up Benjy."

He dropped a light kiss on her forehead. "This isn't over."

"I certainly hope not."

She rested her head against his chest. She'd been in this position a thousand times before—hugging him when she was happy and crying on his shoulder when her life had shattered. Shane was always there for her. He was her rock.

But this moment felt different. Instead of clinging to him, she caressed his back, tracing her fingertips along his spine. She was aware, suddenly aware, that her best friend was a desirable man. His scent aroused her. Through his deputy uniform shirt, she heard the beating of his heart as a primal rhythm, summoning her.

Over the years, she'd seen the way other women threw themselves at Shane. Angela knew he was hot; she'd have to be blind not to notice how handsome he was. But she never imagined that he would be her lover.

He took her shoulders and held her apart from him. The blue of his eyes intoxicated her. She stared at his lips, wanting another kiss or two…or twenty.

"Angela," he said, calling her back to reality. "You're still my buddy. Understand?"

"Mmm." At the moment, friendship wasn't the first thing on her mind. "Tell me about those dreams."

"Can't. It's a guy thing."

She teased, "You fantasized about me. You think I'm pretty. You think I'm sexy."

He kissed the smirk off her lips, leaving her breathless. Then it was his turn to laugh. "I think you're a brat. Just as you've always been."

"Life goes on."

As they climbed down the hill and got back into his car, she wondered how her new vision of Shane would alter their relationship. Earlier, she'd been worried that Benjy would see anger and frustration in her manner. Her son would probably notice that she was glowing like a hot ember.

She tore her gaze away from Shane and stared through the car window as they approached the horse ranch. Beside the road, a log fence enclosed a huge field. Tucked into the pine forest that descended from the rocky foothills was a two-story house and a couple of outbuildings that she assumed were stables. Several horses lounged beside a trough like office workers taking a break at the water cooler.

The man who owned this ranch, Calvin Pratt, was an old friend of Shane's family and the head of a huge extended family. He had six of his grandchildren—ranging in age from three to twelve—staying with him for the summer, and he had a live-in housekeeper to help take care of them. Angela couldn't have asked for a better place to leave her son.

"You're quiet," Shane said.

Uncomfortable silences had never been a problem before.

Trying to slip back into friendship mode, she said, "I called Yvonne from the courthouse. I figured I should take the chance to use a phone since you disabled my cell and won't let me use it."

"For your own safely," he said.

"Yvonne told me that everything at Waffles is fine. They were already prepared for me to be gone for a couple of weeks on my honeymoon."

"You were going to Baja to swim with dolphins."

"Not my number one choice." She felt herself begin to loosen up. When all was said and done, he was still Shane. Her best friend. "Neil said I'd love Baja. Ha! He probably wanted to push me off a cliff onto jagged rocks."

"What did Yvonne have to say about the wedding?"

"A lot. After we took off, she drove across town and went to the chapel."

She'd made it her business to be present, mostly because she took a perverse delight in seeing Neil brought down. If Angela had listened to her friend, she never would have agreed to Neil's proposal.

"What happened?"

"Prentice stood at the front of the chapel and announced that the wedding was off. Yvonne said he made it sound like I'd had a nervous breakdown."

"I'll bet she set the record straight," he said. "Yvonne isn't exactly shy."

"She marched down the aisle—which she said was decorated very nicely with daisy bouquets and ribbons. Then she told everybody to save their get-well cards because I was absolutely fine, and I had a very good reason to call off the wedding. Neil had deceived me."

"Ouch," Shane said. "When one party accuses the other of deception, most people assume infidelity was involved."

"Oh, I'm sure that's what they thought, especially those with dirty minds."

And she had no desire to set the record straight. Explaining about Dr. Prentice and the DNA nightmare wasn't something she was looking forward to. She continued, "Later, Yvonne made arrangements to have all the food that was already prepared and paid for at the reception dinner to be delivered to homeless shelters. I was glad to hear that."

"What about the rest of it? Any regrets?"

"Only that I agreed to marry Neil in the first place."

In that doomed relationship, she'd gotten it so wrong. Could she trust her judgment when it came to Shane? The last thing she wanted was to make another heart-wrenching mistake.

AFTER SHANE DROPPED HER and Benjy off at the cabin, Angela had time to think. When she needed to concentrate, she cooked. Using the meager supplies they'd purchased at the local market, she baked pies and cakes for the gang at the courthouse.

Benjy acted as sous-chef, washing veggies and helping her add ingredients. "A pinch of salt," she said.

He poured a bit from the shaker into his little hand and held it up so she could see. "This much?"

"Perfect," she said.

He threw the salt into the mixture with a flourish. Then he adjusted the brim of the cowboy hat that appeared to be a permanent fixture on his head. "I'm not big enough to ride on the horses by myself."

"Not yet," she agreed.

"But the grandpa let me sit on the saddle with him. And I got to hold the reins. Grandpa's name is Calvin, like Calvin Coolidge." Benjy made the immediate reference, but instead of his usual listing of all presidents before and after Coolidge, he said, "I love horses. Mustangs are wild horses."

"How many does Calvin have?"

He yawned. "A whole bunch."

She shifted from baking to preparing dinner—chicken cacciatore and a creamy, bacon-flavored potato salad that would work for lunch on the following day. Benjy kept up with her, even though he was obviously tired. Tonight, he'd fall into bed early. She and Shane would have some privacy.

Her gaze drifted toward the hide-a-bed sofa in the living room where Shane had been sleeping, and she imagined the two of them lying there naked and tangled up in the quilts and sheets that were neatly folded on the floor.

Apparently, Shane had nothing on her when it came to fantasies. She could hardly wait for this daydream to become reality.

Holding her desires in check, she concentrated on everyday tasks, finishing the preparations for dinner. When Shane returned to the cabin, Benjy told him all about his adventures at the horse ranch. By the time they finished their meal, it was obvious that her son was tired. By eight-thirty, he was in bed. She sat beside him, holding his little hand.

He yawned. "Mommy, are you going to get married?"

She smoothed her hair off his forehead. "I might get married someday. But not to Neil. We don't get along anymore."

That might be the understatement of the century. She still had strong feelings for Neil Revere. All of them negative.

"You don't love him," Benjy said. "Mommies and daddies gotta be in love."

"That's right." She wasn't sure how much to explain. "I bet you have other questions."

"Some." He wrinkled his nose as he snuggled under the homemade patchwork quilt. The artful pattern of blue and green swatches bespoke the excellent craftsmanship of Shane's mother. He'd told Angela that he'd given the quilt to the owner of the cabin in exchange for computer services.

"You can ask me anything, pumpkin."

"Does Neil love me?"

Her automatic response would be to tell her son that everybody loved him, but she wouldn't lie. She couldn't truthfully say anything about Neil's feelings. Though he seemed to love Benjy, his overriding goal was to possess this genius child as evidence of his own cleverness.

"I don't know Neil's feelings," she said honestly. "The reason I called off the wedding was about my feelings. I don't love him."

"Do you love Shane?"

"You bet."

"Are you going to marry Shane?"

A simple question with a complicated answer. She was

ready to take up where they left off this afternoon. More kissing was most certainly in order. But marriage was a whole other thing.

"There are all kinds of love." She picked up his stuffed green dinosaur. "I love this T-Rex because he makes you giggle. And I love ice cream with hot fudge. And I love Yvonne. But I'm not going to marry any of them."

"You can't marry ice cream."

She leaned down to kiss his forehead. "Most of all, I love you."

He flung his little arms around her neck and planted a wet, sloppy kiss on her cheek.

Leaving him to sleep, she closed the door. As she entered the living room, Shane motioned to her. Together, they went outside onto the front porch.

The light from a full moon shone on the surrounding pine trees, chokecherry bushes and rocks. She went to the railing, and Shane stood beside her.

"I was on the computer," he said, "and I couldn't help overhearing what you said to Benjy. Nice job. You didn't lie, but you didn't say too much. You're a good mom."

"You heard Benjy ask if I'd marry you."

"I've wondered the same thing myself. I get along better with you than any other woman I've ever known. You're not half-bad to look at. And you're a great cook."

"If we were living in the 1950s, that's all you'd need for a wife."

"What's different about the 2010s?"

"Check any dating Web site and you'll find a million questions that indicate compatibility, goals, accomplishments and so on." She gave him a playful jab in the ribs. "Not to mention sex."

"Are you propositioning me?"

She looked him up and down. "I sure as hell am."

Chapter Eighteen

For a long time, Shane had admired Angela from afar. He remembered the day Tom introduced them, remembered the way her nose crinkled when she laughed, remembered the daisy she'd stuck into her ponytail. A pretty girl. That went without saying. But Angela had more than a bright smile and a trim body. When he looked in her eyes, he saw an unexpected depth of character, and he couldn't help but wonder what kind of storms she'd weathered in her young life.

From the start, she'd had an effect on Tom. He quit drinking and signed up for AA. He turned into a responsible man and a good husband. Shane had never seen his cousin happier, and he'd wished Tom and Angela the best. He'd taught himself not to yearn for her.

After Tom died, Angela had needed Shane as a friend; her heart had been too broken to think of him in any other way. And they had grieved together.

At the point when he'd begun to hope there might be something more than friendship between them, she brought a new man into her life: Benjy.

When she'd told him that she was getting married to Neil, he'd finally given up hope and accepted that Angela would never be his.

Now she stood before him and demanded the intimacy

that he'd always wanted. In the moonlight, her eyes shimmered. The summer breeze tossed the pine boughs, and the distance between them seemed to shrink as though they were being blown closer together.

He stroked her cheek, pushed a strand of hair behind her ear and said, "I want you to be sure about this."

"I know what you mean." Her voice was breathless, as though she'd just finished a ten-mile run. "Are we moving too fast?"

"We've known each other for seven years," he drawled. "Doesn't seem like a rush to me."

"What if this goes wrong? Oh, Shane. You have to promise me that you'll never stop being my friend. I can't imagine what my life would be like without you."

When she clasped his arm, her touch set off a chemical chain reaction that felt like an adrenaline surge. It was all he could do to restrain himself.

He took her hand and raised it to his lips. Her fingers trembled. He promised, "You'll never get rid of me."

"What if I'm rebounding?"

"What?"

"A rebound," she said. "When one relationship ends, there's a tendency to jump into another before you've resolved all your feelings. It's like a fling."

"Did you read about this in one of those online surveys?"

"Rebounding is a valid issue."

He wished he could take all the self-help articles in the world and torch them in a huge bonfire. "Okay, let's talk about your unresolved feelings for Neil."

She made a sour face. "I don't like him, don't respect him and he scares me a little bit."

"Sounds about right," he said.

"It does." She nodded. "Nothing unresolved there."

"And when we kissed, did it feel like a fling?"

She moved closer. "It felt right. I want to be with you, Shane. Maybe I always have."

That was all the affirmation he needed. He gathered her into his arms and kissed her. He took his time, lingering on her mouth. His hand slid inside her sweater and climbed her slender torso. She was slim but solid with the well-toned muscles of an athlete. At the same time, her curves were one hundred percent feminine. Her hips flared from her waist. When he cupped the fullness of her breast, she made a soft moaning sound that faded into a purr.

Savoring every moment, he opened his eyes and gazed into her lovely face. "Do you know that your eyes look different depending on your mood?"

"People have mentioned that before."

"I've always wondered what color your eyes were when you made love."

"And?"

"Darkest green. Like jade." He took her hand. "Come with me."

She glanced back at the cabin. "I can't leave Benjy."

"We're not going far. And the security alarm is set."

He hadn't wanted the first time they made love to be on a hide-a-bed with her son in the next room. This night would be special. Even if he couldn't treat her to satin sheets and a king-size bed, he'd give her starlight and the fresh scent of pine.

Ten yards up the hill behind the cabin, he'd assembled a nest of sleeping bags inside a circle of trees with a granite stone for a headboard.

She jumped into the center of the sleeping bags. "You were pretty sure I'd say yes."

"From the way you kissed me this afternoon, I had

reason to hope." He stretched out beside her. "But I never take your decisions for granted."

"I'm not capricious."

"But you're not predictable, either. That's one of the things I like about you."

She reached down and started efficiently unbuttoning his shirt. "Don't make it sound like I'm some exotic creature. You know I'm practical and hardworking."

"Stop." He stayed her fingers. "You, Angela, are a force of nature. Exotic doesn't begin to describe you. You're more rare than an orchid. More precious than diamonds."

She gave a snort and sat back on her heels. In a few quick moves, she peeled off her sweater and pulled her T-shirt up and over her head, revealing her no-nonsense zip-front sports bra. "I'm a cook."

"Chef," he corrected her. "You're an artist."

From the businesslike way she was tearing off her clothes, he could tell that she hadn't been properly seduced. The time had come for him to take charge and show her how truly special she was. He rolled over her and pinned her shoulders on the sleeping bag. "Let me undress you."

She gave him a curious look. "But it's always so clumsy when—"

He silenced her with a kiss. Slowly, he lavished attention on the sensitive parts of her body. Her earlobes. The hollow at the base of her throat. The soft skin on the inside of her elbow. And her breasts. Through the fabric of her bra, he teased her nipples into tight buds. When he finally unzipped the front of her bra, she gave a feral yelp that made him glad they weren't in the living room of the cabin.

Her impatience turned to arousal as she responded to the slow, deliberate rhythm of his lovemaking. Her hands explored his body. She was aggressive, as though she'd been programmed to follow certain steps. Though his need for her was rising to an intense level, he paused. He didn't want to be another lover. He would be her *only* lover.

Straddling her hips, he caught both her hands in his grasp. "Lie still, Angela."

She wriggled beneath him. "Why?"

Her long hair fanned out. "I want to see you. To appreciate how beautiful you are."

Her eyes, her jade eyes, gazed up at him, and she smiled. "Do I live up to your fantasy?"

"You're better than I dreamed."

He lay beside her on his back, looking up through the trees at the shimmering pinpricks of distant stars. When she linked her hand with him, a bond formed between them. They were the only people on the planet.

"I like what you said," she whispered, "about seeing me. I want to be seen."

"After all these years, it seems like we ought to know everything about each other. But there's always more."

"Another mood." She sighed. "A secret we haven't yet shared."

"This night is only the start."

And they took their time. Each touch was a new discovery as though neither of them had ever made love before. Their passion developed by degrees until the urgency overwhelmed him, and he lost himself in her.

UNDER THE DOWN COMFORTER he'd brought from the cabin, Angela snuggled against his naked chest. Her body trembled with delicious aftershocks from their lovemaking. She felt as if she'd eaten a seven-course gourmet dinner prepared by a master chef, worthy of the coveted three-star Michelin rating.

She'd always assumed that Shane was a good lover, but tonight surpassed anything she could fantasize about.

When he reached behind the granite rock beside them and pulled out a picnic basket, she wasn't surprised. The man had finesse. He unpacked a bottle of burgundy and two glasses.

"You thought of everything," she said.

"I want the best for you."

When he uncorked the wine, she noticed that he'd gotten wineglasses. She held one up. "We didn't have these glasses in the cabin before."

"I picked them up in town."

The goose-down comforter covered him from the waist down, but his chest was bare. He had just the right amount of springy black hair. As far as she could tell, he didn't have an ounce of flab. He was all muscle, all man.

Though the night breeze cooled her back and shoulders, she didn't feel the need for a sweater. The heat of their passion still kept her warm. "What else have you picked up?"

"Is there something I need to get?"

"I'm asking if you've done any more investigating."

"Are you sure you want to talk about this?"

"It's not the usual pillow talk." She gestured to the surrounding forest. "But this isn't a usual pillow. The sooner we figure out what's going on with Prentice and Neil, the sooner we can get back to our normal lives."

"I don't have much to go on." He poured the wine and handed her a glass. "I dropped off the swab for Benjy's DNA profile. And, here's a bonus, I can have Neil tested as well. They took DNA when he was booked."

"Is that standard procedure?"

"It's within the parameters of the law. We ought to have results in a couple of days."

She held up her glass, aware that she was completely

naked and not feeling in the least self-conscious. When he touched his glass with hers, she said, "To the first night."

"But not the last," he concluded her thought.

The wine aroused her taste buds and slid down her throat. All her senses seemed to be heightened. And her mind felt sharp. "What else are you working on?"

"You told me that Prentice has a cabin in this area, and I want to locate it."

"Why?" She grinned over the rim of her glass. "Are you hoping to find skeletons in his closet?"

"I won't know what I'm looking for until I see it. There's a lot that can be learned from the way a person lives." He licked a drop of wine from his lips. "When I was at the courthouse, I checked some property records. Prentice's house in Aspen is a multimillion-dollar chalet. Plus, he owns a smaller Aspen house that he rents out. And another in Glenwood Springs that's also occupied by renters."

It wasn't unusual for longtime mountain residents to own several properties. Deals became available, and people bought at a good price. In the West, land was always considered a good investment. "But Prentice doesn't have a cabin in this area?"

"Not in his name."

"What else are you investigating?"

"Carlson. I want to find out how much dirty work he's done for Neil."

"What have you turned up so far?" she asked.

"Not much. His academic records are marginal. Right now, he's only taking a part-time course load. He sure as hell doesn't seem like somebody Neil would handpick as his protégé. How much do you know about him?"

She'd never paid much attention to Carlson. He was ubiquitous, part of the background. "He's a snowboarder. Prentice said that he knew Carlson in Aspen."

"A couple of years ago," Shane said, "Carlson had a drunk and disorderly charge in Aspen. Since then, all he's had are a couple of traffic citations."

The pine boughs rustled in the wind, and she gave a little shiver. "It's chilly."

"Come over here and lean on me. I'll keep you warm."

She rested against his chest and pulled the comforter up to cover herself. With Shane holding her, she felt as if she was wrapped inside a cozy cocoon.

"The third issue I'm looking into," he said, "is Neil's mother."

"What does his mother have to do with anything?"

"Have you ever heard of the 'curious incident of the dog in the night'?"

She sipped her wine. "Doesn't ring any bells."

"Not a Sherlock Holmes fan, huh? Well, Holmes solved a case based on the fact that while the crime was taking place the dogs did *not* bark. No barking meant the dogs knew the intruder."

She twisted her head to look up at him. Moonlight shone on the strong, masculine planes of his face. In his features, she saw a younger version of Shane—a boy who savored Sherlock Holmes adventures. "I didn't know you liked detective stories."

"It was one of the reasons I became a deputy. I liked the idea of putting together the clues and coming up with a solution that led to an arrest."

"Are you sure you want to leave that job and work for PRESS?"

"Oh, yeah. Real-life law enforcement seldom involves a mystery. It's pretty much cut-and-dried. You see the bad guy and lock him up."

"So this chance to investigate must be interesting for you."

"I'm pretty sure that once we have all the pieces, the puzzle won't be that complicated," he said. "Anyway, Neil's mother is like the dog not barking. Nobody in his family says much about her, and that makes me think she might be important. What can you tell me about Janice Revere?"

"She and Roger are divorced. Obviously. And I guess it was a really bloody separation. Neil is estranged from her. Prentice told me that she has serious mental problems and has been hospitalized as a schizophrenic."

"That's not what I heard from Dr. Em. She recalled something about Neil's mother working as a psychiatrist at a hospital back east. Anyway, I looked her up online and came up with several women named Janice Revere. None were the right age."

"She could be using her maiden name."

"Or she could be married again. Dr. Em didn't know anything else about her."

Angela didn't bother wondering about why Prentice would lie about Neil's mother. Or why Neil never revealed anything about his estrangement from her. The two of them had done nothing but lie. "What's next?"

"I'll ask around and see if I can gather more information."

"Can I help?"

He gave her a squeeze and kissed the top of her head. "The number one priority is keeping you and Benjy safe. Neil's going to be out of jail by tomorrow, and he might come looking for you."

"But I have a restraining order."

As soon as the words left her lips, she knew a piece of paper wouldn't stop Neil from doing exactly as he wanted. He'd meant what he said about not letting her go.

She'd like to believe that she could handle herself, but when he'd lashed out at her in the parking lot, she'd been startled. Never before had she been struck by a man. The only fights she'd gotten into were playground shoving matches.

His blow had chipped away at her self-confidence, even though it hadn't caused any actual physical harm. Neil had shown himself to be capable of physical violence, and that scared her.

"This cabin is secure," Shane said. "But I don't want you to be here alone. During the day, it's best if you and Benjy stay with Calvin at the horse ranch where there are plenty of people around."

She finished her wine and set the glass aside. Turning around in his embrace, she wrapped her arms around him. "But I want to be with you."

"As much as possible."

"And as often as possible."

He kissed her, and she tasted wine on his lips. Though she had been completely satisfied, she wanted to make love again. She wished this night could last forever.

Chapter Nineteen

Over the next couple of days, Angela settled into a routine. First, she'd go for a morning run on the gravel road outside the cabin. Then, Shane would take her and Benjy to the horse ranch where they'd spend most of the day. After dinner, the night belonged to her and Shane.

This morning she'd already done her exercise and showered. In the cabin kitchen, she prepared cheese omelets to go with the muffins she'd made the night before, and her mind wandered. Last night, they'd made love beside the creek, bathed in moonlight and serenaded by the rush of water.

When they had climbed the hill back to the cabin so they'd be nearby in case Benjy woke up, they had seen intruders: a family of elk crossed in front of the cabin at a stately pace.

Though it had been close to midnight, she hadn't been ready for sleep, so she made them chamomile tea flavored with a stick of cinnamon. They went onto the porch to sip and talk. After all these years, it didn't seem as if they'd have much to say, but there were endless stories of their pasts and even more plans for the future. He encouraged her to write that cookbook of her breakfast recipes—something Neil would have put down as unimportant. And she promised to fly with him as soon as he was a certified helicopter pilot.

Her fears about losing him as a friend had been utterly unfounded. Their friendship hadn't changed; it had grown.

The morning light through the cabin window held the promise of another beautiful day. Though there was still much to be settled, she was beginning to feel safe. After he got out of jail, Neil hadn't tried to contact her. Nor had Prentice. Their precaution of keeping their location a secret seemed to be working.

She looked up from the stove as Shane and Benjy tromped through the front door of the cabin. Benjy dashed to the table. "I'm starving, Mommy."

"You're just in time." She prepared his plate and carried it to the coffee table in the living room, which was the only place they could all sit together and eat in this small cabin.

In the kitchen, Shane dished up his own food. He gave her a little kiss on the cheek before he joined Benjy. She liked the way their intimacy spilled over into their regular life. Casual kisses, hugs and holding hands felt perfectly natural, and Benjy seemed to accept their deepening relationship without question.

Her son was doing well in this mountain environment. Wearing his ever-present cowboy hat, he blended in with the other kids at the horse ranch. The only place he was a know-it-all was in the kitchen at the ranch house.

Angela had taken over the cooking chores to help out at the ranch, which was fine with her. She preferred keeping her hands busy and enjoyed coming up with new recipes for farm-fresh produce and the lusciously marbled beef from a nearby ranch. Every afternoon, she baked something sweet—cookies or a pie—and the children gathered around. Benjy was the self-appointed supervisor, telling all the other kids how to hold a spoon and how to measure.

She sat at the table and looked at her two men. "This is nice," she said. "Being together. Having breakfast. I could do this forever, until I grow old and gray."

Shane shot her a glance. "Speak for yourself, Grandma."

Benjy laughed. "Yeah, Grandma."

"We've got a lot to do today," Shane said. "I just got a phone call, and I'm going to need your help, Angela. I want you to come into town with me."

She looked at Benjy. "Will you be okay at the ranch?"

"I gotta be there," he said. "One of the mares is having a baby, and I have to help."

"Well, then, I guess I won't be missed."

She wondered about Shane's phone call. It was time for the DNA profiles for Benjy and Neil to have come back from the lab. Though she was fairly sure that she wouldn't like the results, she needed answers.

AFTER THEY DROPPED OFF Benjy, Shane held the car door for Angela and went around his Land Rover to slide behind the steering wheel. Though he was wearing his uniform, he doubted he'd be doing much work for Clear Creek County. His status as a lame-duck deputy allowed him free rein to pursue his investigation into Neil and Prentice.

Due to budget restrictions, the higher-ups had already decided that his position wouldn't be filled after he left to work for PRESS. The rest of the deputies said they'd miss him, but were also relieved that none of them would be laid off to trim costs.

As they drove away from the ranch, Angela peppered him with questions. "Who called you this morning? It was the lab, wasn't it? Should we contact Eve to interpret the DNA profiles?"

"Sorry," he said. "My call this morning wasn't about the DNA."

She flopped back in her seat. "Thank goodness."

"I thought you were anxious to find out."

"Of course, I want to know." Her slender hand rested near her throat as she exhaled a giant sigh. "At the same time, I don't."

"Because you have to face the problem and deal with it."

She nodded. "If the phone call wasn't about the DNA, what was it?"

"I've got a location for Prentice's cabin." He'd wasted a lot of time with computer searches, interviews with the county assessor's office and phone calls. Yesterday, he drove all the way to Fairplay in Park County to search through property records. "I'm guessing that this place is where Prentice goes to get away from it all. His hideaway. His name isn't on any of the records."

"If his name isn't on it, how did you figure it out?"

"The old-fashioned way," he said. "I talked to our local postmistress, and she referred me to somebody else and somebody else. This morning, she finally got information and called me. One of the rural delivery drivers had a note to deliver a package addressed to Dr. Prentice at a cabin belonging to J. Stilton."

"The name doesn't ring any bells," she said. "Why did you want me to come along?"

Partly because he wanted to spend more time with her. When they were apart, she filled his mind and he couldn't wait to get back to her. "I need your help to figure out what Neil and Prentice are up to. Our easygoing lifestyle won't stay this way forever."

Her eyes widened in alarm. "Have there been threats? Is there something you're not telling me?"

For a moment, he took his eyes off the road and met her gaze. Honesty had always been the cornerstone of their relationship. Though he had dedicated himself to protecting her, he wouldn't lie to her. "I'm not keeping secrets, and I never will. If there's a need for worry, you'll know about it."

"Good." She emphasized the word with a nod. "You don't have to treat me like a precious hothouse orchid."

"You are precious, but you're sturdy, too."

"A sturdy orchid?"

"A daisy," he said. "I want you to know that Neil hasn't given up. He and Prentice have both been sighted in this area. I reckon they're doing the same thing we are, but in reverse. They're trying to find our hideout."

"But they can't," she said. "Right?"

"I sure as hell hope not."

Though he didn't think Neil would physically harm her or Benjy, he wouldn't be surprised by a kidnapping scheme. Neil was arrogant enough to think that if he got Angela alone, he could still win her back.

"Tell me how to help," she said. "What are we looking for at this cabin?"

"You know these people better than I do. That's why I wanted you with me."

He concentrated on the road. Though he knew his way around Clear Creek County, he'd never been in this area and he was glad he had the GPS navigator to show him the way. Rural routes could be tricky; there were few road signs or markings to show where you were.

When they got close, he started reading the names on mailboxes at the side of the road. On a battered metal box, he could just make out the name *Stilton*.

Angela saw it, too. "There."

A fence that had once been white marked off a property that looked to be about two acres. A gray, ranch-style house with a sloped roof stood at the end of the gravel driveway. The detached garage was almost as big as the house.

"Doesn't look like anybody's home," he said. "No cars. But they could be parked in that garage."

"The house and grounds seem too dilapidated for Prentice. He's got expensive taste."

He drove to a crossroads and turned. Behind a stand of trees, he parked the car. "Let's do a little trespassing."

They made their way across another larger property that also appeared to be deserted. Though the forest was sparse and plain, the mountain views were attractive. He reckoned this area was filled mostly with vacation homes that were used only in summer or for weekend getaways. Or they could be rentals left vacant by the sluggish economy. Not many people could afford to live in solitude; they needed jobs and the price of gas made it impractical to make the commute from the mountains.

The morning sun beat down on his back. He could feel himself starting to sweat. Breaking into the Stilton house wasn't the way he usually pursued his duties. As a duly appointed law enforcement official, he could justify his actions as part of an ongoing investigation. Dr. Prentice had committed fraud many years ago when Angela was born. But Shane knew he was stepping outside the boundaries of legality into a gray area.

A tall spruce tree stood beside the house, and he crept into its shadow. Angela was right beside him. "What do we do now?" she asked.

"We hope that Prentice isn't sitting behind the door with a shotgun."

"He'd never dirty his hands with something so crude," she said. "But Carlson would."

Shane moved across the dried prairie grass to the back-door and tried to turn the knob. The good news was that Prentice didn't appear to have an alarm system. The bad news? The door was locked.

Angela peeked into the window beside the door. "This is a kitchen. I can hardly see through this filthy glass, but it's kind of cute inside. There's a vintage honey bear cookie jar."

He could have kicked down the door, but it was smarter to use finesse so Prentice wouldn't know they'd been here. He squatted down to eye level with the lock and took out a set of picks.

She hovered beside him. "Interesting skill. Are you a deputy or a cat burglar?"

"We patrol a lot of areas with empty houses," he said as he maneuvered the picks. "It's handy to be able to get inside."

After a few minutes, he had the lock unfastened. As Angela had noted, the kitchen seemed pleasant and wel-coming, with cherry-patterned wallpaper and red vinyl covers on the breakfast nook. Though dust lay thick on the windowsill, the counter had been wiped down. "Someone has been here recently."

Angela gave no sign of fear as she explored. Her first move was to open the refrigerator. "Whoever has been stay-ing here likes beer. Three six-packs."

The circular oak table in the dining area was covered with dust, and he saw footprints on the dusty hardwood floor. The pattern was common to work boots. Not the kind of footwear he expected Prentice to wear. Nothing about the furniture or the lamps or the knickknacks suggested the expensive taste of Dr. Prentice.

He pulled up the top on a rolltop desk. There was nothing inside but a couple of advertising flyers. He was beginning to think they'd come to the wrong house when Angela took a framed photograph off the mantel and studied it. "That's Neil."

The picture showed a skinny kid, probably eleven or twelve years old, dressed in a soccer uniform and proudly displaying a trophy. "How can you tell it's him?"

"He has the same picture at his house."

Other photos showed Neil as a toddler and in a Halloween costume. "There's nothing about the older Neil. You'd think somebody like Prentice would find more value in graduation pictures than in kid stuff."

Angela turned on her heel and strolled around the room. "I don't think he lives here. This place looks like it was decorated by a woman."

"A woman named Stilton."

"Prentice never married," she said. "I always thought it was odd for an ob-gyn who specialized in fertility treatments. He never had children of his own."

"He could have had a mistress, and this was her house." He went down the hallway. The doors stood open to two bedrooms and a bath. A rumpled comforter covered one of the bare mattresses. "This bed has been slept in."

"Recently?" she asked.

"I can't say for sure. From all the dust, I'd guess that this house has been closed up for a long time. But it's been lived in."

"By somebody who likes beer and didn't bother to sweep all the floors. That doesn't seem like Prentice or Neil."

He raised an eyebrow. "Are they both good house-keepers?"

"They wouldn't tolerate the dirt." She glanced with disgust at the floors and the dirty windows. "Not that either of them would pick up a broom. They'd hire somebody to get the place tidied up."

He'd been smart to bring Angela along; she noticed things that he wouldn't have seen. "You know," he said, "if Prentice used this place as a hideaway for his mistress, it would explain all the secrecy. He wouldn't want his name on this property."

"But that doesn't make sense. He's a single man. He doesn't need to hide his relationship."

"Unless she was married." He put the pieces together. "A married woman with an interest in Neil."

"Oh, my God. He was having an affair with Neil's mother."

Shane had been drifting toward the same conclusion. Prentice and Shane's father had been lifelong friends. Prentice would want to hide his involvement with the mysterious Mrs. Revere. Now that he had a name for the woman— Janice Stilton—he could locate her. "Do you think Neil found out?"

"If he did, why would he be friends with Prentice?"

"You met his father," he said. "Roger Revere isn't a real warm and likable guy."

"And Neil would blame his mother." She gave a snort of disgust. "That's why they were estranged and he refused to talk about her."

Tires crunched on the gravel outside the house. Someone was coming. Shane went to the bedroom window and looked out. He saw a black truck.

Chapter Twenty

Before Angela had a chance to think, Shane rushed her through the house. "Somebody's coming. Run."

She dashed into the living room. Her foot slipped and she stumbled. She tried to catch herself on the back of the wood chair beside the desk, but she was off balance. Both she and the chair hit the floor with a crash. Panic raced through her. If anyone was standing outside the front door, they'd hear.

As she scrambled to her feet, Shane yanked the chair upright and shoved it toward the desk. She would have straightened it out, but there wasn't time.

He grabbed her hand and pulled her through the kitchen and into the backyard. He closed the door. Under his breath, he muttered, "We should have covered our tracks."

"What do you mean?"

"The chair is off kilter. I opened the rolltop desk. You moved photos on the mantel."

"Do you think they'll notice?"

"Let's hope not."

Instead of racing back the way they came, he signaled her to be quiet and eased toward the side of the house. He was moving in the direction opposite the way they'd come when they approached the cabin. What was he thinking? Did he want to be caught?

Following him closer than his own shadow, she bumped into his back when he halted at the front of the house.

"What are you doing?" she whispered.

"We're okay. He didn't hear us inside the house because he was parking in the garage."

"Who is it?"

"Carlson." Shane pressed his back against the side of the house. "Quiet."

She stood beside him. Her heart thumped so loudly that she couldn't hear anything else. Fear ripped through her, and she hated that she was afraid of Carlson. During the whole time she'd known him, Neil's protégé had been a nonpresence. He'd faded into the wallpaper, seldom speaking and never making a scene.

But Carlson had put her through hell with his late-at-night whispered messages and his creepy stalking. He was probably responsible for slashing her wedding gown, and she knew that he'd do *anything* for Neil.

She heard the front door of the house slam. To Shane, she whispered, "Now do we run?"

"There's something I need to check out. Stick with me."

He dodged across the open space that separated the house and the garage, frequently looking over his shoulder to make sure Carlson hadn't spotted them. At the three-car garage, he opened the side door, pulled her inside and closed it.

Darkness surrounded them. Her nostrils twitched with the stink of grime and oil. Shane hit the light switch by the door, and a couple of bare bulbs cast a dim light.

Against the back wall was a workbench with an array of tools. Underneath were two five-gallon gas cans. She looked past the typical clutter that accumulates in a garage—trash cans and stuffed black garbage bags, an old television set, a broken rocking chair, a snowblower.

At the far end of the garage was a black truck—the same type of vehicle that had killed Tom five years ago.

The sight of it shocked her. *Was this the same truck?* Her throat tightened; she was unable to breathe. In her mind, she replayed the moment of his death. The clock read ten twenty-three. Through her phone, she heard the violent, fatal crash and Tom's whispered last words: *Love you, too.* Then silence.

Shane crossed the garage and went to the front of the truck. His hand rested on the fender. He leaned close, studying the joint between the fender and the door. When he looked at her, his gaze was stricken.

In a deathly calm voice, he said, "It's a '97 or '98. This fender has been replaced. The paint doesn't match the rest of the truck. There's no way of knowing if this is the original bumper or not."

This was the truck. She knew it. She sensed it.

Furious, she charged forward. With both fists, she hammered at the wall of the truck bed. She lashed out again and again as though she could destroy this damn thing with her bare hands. Overwhelmed with incomprehensible rage, she staggered backward until she bumped against the workbench. Her hands flew up to cover her face.

She should have been sobbing, but the tears didn't come. Her eyes squeezed shut. Her vision went dark. She could see the headlights of the truck coming toward her, not slowing down. The truck careened, faster and faster.

Shane wrapped her in his embrace. Wordlessly, he held her. She knew he was struggling, too. She could feel the tension in his arms. Tom had been his cousin, his best friend.

"I should have known it was Carlson," she said. "As

soon as we figured out that he was stalking me, I should have known. He always woke me up at ten twenty-three. On the night when you came to the house, I thought I saw truck lights through the kitchen window."

Carlson had been acting out Tom's death, night after night. He used that tragedy to haunt her.

She shivered and buried her face against Shane's chest. "You have to arrest him."

"First, I need proof." He gently stroked her back. "This truck says something to you and me, but I doubt there's going to be anything in the way of forensic evidence. It was five years ago, and the truck has been repaired."

"What about records of the repair job? Receipts from a body shop? There's got to be something."

"There is," he assured her. "Carlson won't get away with murder. And when he confesses, I'll arrest the man who put him up to it."

Carlson wasn't acting alone. He was a stooge—a stupid, pathetic toady who was capable only of following instructions. "It was Neil, wasn't it?"

"Neil or Prentice. Or both of them."

The whole terrible plot became clear. Neil and Prentice had manipulated Tom so he would insist on having their embryos frozen. Then they killed Tom to get control of her. She'd readily agreed to the IVF procedure. "I fell right into their trap."

"Don't blame yourself. You had no way of knowing what they were doing."

"Because I didn't know about the Prentice-Jantzen study, didn't know that I had been genetically engineered."

Eve had told her that there were only two females from that study. Prentice needed her to create the second generation: Benjy. She shook herself. "They can't get away with this."

"They won't," he assured her. "They're all going to jail."

Those were the words she wanted to hear. She wanted to know that Tom's death would be avenged.

ON THE DRIVE BACK TO THE sheriff's office, Angela fidgeted in the passenger seat, wishing she could make Shane's car move faster. "Are you sure the deputy you left watching the house won't let Carlson get away?"

"You heard my instructions. Don't let anyone leave but if somebody else shows up, don't stop them. Let them enter."

"Why do we have to go to the courthouse?"

"I need to coordinate the evidence, inform the sheriff and get a warrant. I'm making this arrest by the book. The worst thing that could happen now is to have these guys get off on a technicality."

Earlier, she hadn't wanted to press charges against Prentice because he could afford a dream team of lawyers. But this was different. They were talking about murder—Tom's murder.

She looked over at Shane. With his jaw set and his eyes focused straight ahead, he looked like a man on a mission— strong and determined. "I can always trust you to do the right thing."

"It's my job."

"For now," she said. "But you're not going to be a deputy much longer."

"And this arrest is one hell of a fine way to end my law enforcement career. I'll finally get justice for Tom."

A rush of gratitude went through her. She was so glad that he was in her life. In the midst of sorrow and rage, Shane had always stood beside her. The love she felt for him grew deeper every day, and she wanted to tell him what was in her heart.

But now probably wasn't the best time.

He glanced toward her. "When we get to the courthouse, I'll arrange for someone to take you to the horse ranch so you can be with Benjy."

"I want to come with you."

"It's police business."

She had a stake in what happened—perhaps the biggest stake, but she didn't want to get in the way. "Is there anything I can do?"

"Talk to Neil's mother."

Shane's phone calls to headquarters had already produced results. A search of records showed that Stilton was the maiden name of Janice Revere's mother. After her divorce, Janice Revere used the name Janice Stilton until she remarried and added a hyphen. She was now Janice Stilton-Parke, and she worked as a psychologist at a private clinic in Vermont.

Shane said, "I don't think she'll be useful as a witness. She left Colorado twenty-four years ago."

"When Neil was only twelve." Though Angela couldn't imagine how any mother could leave her child, she wouldn't pass judgment until she'd heard the whole story.

SHORTLY AFTER THEY ARRIVED at the courthouse, Shane directed her into an office that wasn't being used. There was an empty desk, a chair and a telephone. He placed a piece of paper with the phone numbers for Neil's mother on the desk.

He sat her in the swivel chair, turned her toward him and leaned down to kiss her on the lips.

She pulled back. "We shouldn't. I don't want people to get the wrong idea."

"Too late," he drawled. "Most people already think we're sleeping together. I mean, we're a couple of consenting adults, staying in a secluded cabin without a television."

"Why does a TV make a difference?"

"I'm easily distracted."

"Are you telling me that you'd find television more interesting than making love?"

"That depends. If we had the satellite sports network, I might be—"

She rose to her feet, held his face in her hands and kissed him hard and long. Just as she felt him beginning to respond, she ended the kiss. "Make no mistake, Shane. I'm way better than ESPN."

He gave her a pat on the butt and headed toward the door. "Take your time with the phone call."

His joking around had been just what she needed to relax. She sat behind the desk and dialed.

When a woman answered, Angela asked, "Is this Janice Stilton-Parke?"

"Yes, it is. Who's calling?"

"My name is Angela Hawthorne. I need to ask you a few questions about your son, Neil Revere. This is very important. Please don't hang up."

"I don't think I can help you." Her voice was calm and reasonable—exactly what Angela would expect from a psychologist. "I'm estranged from my son and haven't seen him in years."

"Neil and I were engaged."

"Past tense," Janice noted. "I have a few minutes, Angela. Go ahead and ask your questions."

It would be the height of cruelty to call this woman out of the blue and tell her that her son had turned into a murderer. Angela chose her words carefully. "When were you divorced from Roger?"

"Over twenty years ago."

"Was there a pre-nup?"

"No, but Roger is a lawyer. He used the courts to his advantage and obtained full custody of Neil. I tried to stay in contact. Made every effort. Until Neil told me he wanted nothing more to do with me."

"Do you remember Dr. Edgar Prentice?"

"Yes." Her answer was clipped, terse.

Angela asked, "What was your relationship with him?"

"Edgar was a friend of Roger's. They knew each other for years, even before we were married."

"Do you own property in Clear Creek County?"

There was a pause. "I suppose my name is on the property. Edgar purchased the land and cabin. He pays all the taxes and bills."

"Did you ever live on that property?"

"You're being very circumspect, Angela. It's not necessary. Long ago, I made peace with the feelings I have about my first marriage and my estrangement from Neil. I was foolish. I made a mistake, and I paid for it."

"The mistake," Angela said. "Was it Dr. Prentice?"

"I had an affair with him. That was why we were so clandestine about the cabin. I didn't want my husband to know that I'd betrayed him. He suspected that I had a lover, but I never told him that I was sleeping with his best friend."

Uncomfortable, Angela stared at the blank wall opposite the desk in the empty office. It wasn't her style to pry into another woman's life, but Janice seemed to be forthcoming and honest. "When did your affair with Prentice start?"

"I know the answer you're looking for, Angela. I never acknowledged this to Neil or his father, but it should have been obvious. They look nothing alike. Over the years, I've followed my son's career. It was no accident that he went into the field of medicine."

Angela knew what was coming next. "Like his father?"

"That's right," Janice said. "Edgar Prentice is Neil's biological father."

Chapter Twenty-One

In the courthouse, Shane paced the hallway outside the sheriff's office while the logistics of Carlson's arrest were being worked out. Since the murder took place in Park County, the sheriff in that jurisdiction needed to be advised. Shane was glad they had good reciprocal relations with Park County. He'd been there just a couple of days ago looking for information about Prentice's cabin.

Five years ago, when Tom was murdered, Shane had frequently conferred with the Park County investigators assigned to the case. He'd studied the photographs of the crime scene and reviewed the meager evidence, including the bloody fingerprint on Tom's SUV.

Five years ago, they found no match for the fingerprint. Since then Carlson had gotten himself arrested in Aspen for being drunk and disorderly. Now his prints were in the system. And Carlson's prints matched those found at the scene of the crime.

Shane had laid out his murder theory for the sheriff who agreed that they should be on the lookout for Prentice and Neil. At the very least, they were witnesses.

Sticking to the letter of the law helped Shane control his need for revenge. The minute he saw that damn truck, he wanted to rip Carlson's head off. That little bastard had killed a good man; he should suffer the ultimate punishment. But Shane didn't want this to end with Carlson. Neil and Prentice were equally culpable.

Down the hallway, he saw Angela leave the office where she'd been talking on the phone. She walked toward him with her head held high. Her cheeks flamed with color. She stepped into his arms and held on tight. Though the shape of her body had become familiar during their nights of lovemaking, the sensation of holding her still amazed him. After all these years, they'd found their fit as lovers.

"How was the phone call?" he asked.

"Tragic. I feel bad for Neil's mother."

"Before you tell me about her, I should show you this." He took an envelope from his back pocket. "The DNA results."

"It's still sealed."

"I thought you should be the one to open it."

She shook her head. "I don't think I can take any more shocks today. You read it and tell me what it says."

He escorted her to the wooden bench against the wall outside the sheriff's office, and he sat close beside her. Her posture was erect, as though her spine were a steel rod. He knew she was tense. If Benjy wasn't her biological child, she might be better off not knowing. "Are you ready for this?"

"Just get it over with."

Using his thumb, he opened the envelope and took out four sheets of paper. One was a copy of Angela's DNA profile that Eve had sent. There were two other similar sheets for Benjy and Neil. Shane didn't have the scientific know-how to interpret the results, but the technician had enclosed a cover letter to explain.

He skimmed the letter until he found the pertinent sentences which he read aloud. "The accuracy is 97.8 percent.

Subject A (Angela) and Subject N (Neil) are the genetic parents of Subject B (Benjy)."

"Neil," she said. "Neil is Benjy's father?"

"Maybe not. It's only 97.8 percent accurate."

"No wonder he was so determined to get custody. Benjy is his son."

"That's the biological part," he said. "As far as I'm concerned, Benjy is the child born from the love between you and Tom. You both planned for him. You went through the frozen embryo process together. He's Tom's boy."

"That's a good way for me to think of it."

But he could tell that she wasn't convinced. The fraud Prentice had perpetrated on her was particularly cruel. He'd lured her and Tom to his clinic, had extracted her egg and fertilized it with Neil's sperm. All without her consent or knowledge.

He held her chin and turned her face toward him. In her eyes, he saw pain and anger and other emotions he couldn't identify. "You're going to be all right with this."

"You don't know the worst part," she said. "Neil's mother had an affair with Prentice. He's Neil's biological father."

And Benjy's grandfather.

IN THE PARKING LOT behind the courthouse, Angela watched as Shane and three other deputies headed toward two vehicles. They'd broken out the bulletproof vests and heavy weaponry. Shane had told her that they were going to arrest Carlson, but he'd be taken to Park County where he'd be formally charged and incarcerated.

Shane strode over to where she was standing. "This is going to be over soon."

"I still don't understand why I can't come with you."

"Taking a murder suspect into custody is official police business. Not a spectator sport."

She leaned close and whispered, "You didn't mind having me along when we broke into the Stilton house."

"And we almost got caught." He handed over the keys to his Land Rover. "Take my car and wait for me at Calvin's horse ranch. But I don't want you driving alone. Get one of the dispatch officers to go with you."

"I don't need a babysitter."

"And you don't need to take risks," he said. "As long as Neil and Prentice are still at large, you're in danger."

One of the deputies motioned to Shane. She knew he had to hurry, but she hated being left behind. Seeing Carlson in handcuffs would bring her much-needed satisfaction. "Please let me come along."

He slapped a cell phone into her hand. "I'll call you and tell you everything that happens."

After giving her a peck on the cheek, he went to join the others. He looked good walking away. She'd always thought his uniform was sexy.

Resigned to her passive role, she juggled the car keys in her hand. In spite of Shane's warning, she figured she could manage the drive to Calvin's ranch by herself. Riding alone would give her time to think and absorb all that had happened today.

She went to his Land Rover and got behind the wheel. After adjusting the seat and the rearview mirror, she fastened her seat belt and drove away from the courthouse. The route to Calvin's horse ranch led away from town into the forest. These untraveled roads were pleasant; she did some of her best thinking when she was driving.

Knowing the truth about Benjy's DNA worried her. Though she took solace in the fact that he was genetically engineered to be a genius, she hated to think that he might inherit Prentice's lack of ethics or Neil's arrogance. Surely, those traits were learned behavior. She couldn't imagine her little guy being cruel in any way.

But Janice Revere must have felt the same way about her son. When Neil rejected her and sided with his father and Prentice, she must have been hurt.

Later, Angela might contact Janice and tell her about Benjy, offer her the chance to know her grandson. Benjy didn't have other grandparents. The closest thing to extended family he had was Shane's parents. And Eve, she reminded herself. Her half sister.

As she took a sharp turn onto a gravel road, the SUV seemed to wobble as though it was unstable.

The cell phone rang and she answered, "Hello, Shane."

"How are you doing?"

"I'm on the way to Calvin's." She decided to tell him the truth. "And I didn't drag anyone along with me. I'm fine."

"Are there any other cars on the road?"

She hadn't been watching the mirrors, but took a glance now. "Nobody in sight. And when did you get to be such a mother hen?"

"I think that happened right after I fell in love with you."

She pulled the phone away from her ear and stared at it. Did he just say that he loved her? He must have because the L-word echoed inside her head. How could he make that declaration over the phone? So casual. So calm.

"Angela, just be careful. If you have any trouble at all, hit the redial button and I'll answer."

Before she could respond, he disconnected the call.

Of course, she loved Shane as a friend. And she loved the way he seduced her. But was she in love with him?

She yanked at the wheel. The ride over this gravel road

was worse than it had ever been before. Something was wrong with this car.

A flat tire.

Her fingers clenched the steering wheel. *No! This can't be happening!* A flat tire led to Tom's death. She wouldn't let them kill her, too. Through the windshield, she saw the surrounding forest. There were no houses in sight. No other cars.

The car jostled wildly. She knew she should pull off onto the shoulder, but her foot wouldn't come off the accelerator. If she could keep going, she wouldn't be stuck here.

In her rearview mirror, she saw another car approaching. Sunlight gleamed on the chrome of the other vehicle. The front grill looked like shark's teeth.

She had to change directions. Couldn't risk leading them to Benjy. She'd rather die than let Neil get his hands on her son. But there was nowhere to turn on this road. No escape.

The other car pulled up to her back bumper. She couldn't outrun him with a flat tire. She had a better chance on foot. Every morning, she'd been running. All that training might pay off.

She swerved, and the other car gave her a little more room. He didn't want to put a dent in his expensive grill. If only she could get some distance, she'd have a better chance.

She unfastened her seat belt and tucked the cell phone into her sports bra. The phone was her only link to Shane. She slammed on the brakes. Shane's Land Rover swiveled to a stop.

Immediately, she threw open the door and dashed around the front of the car. Following her instincts, she sprinted across a rock-strewn open space toward a thick stand of aspen. Pumping hard, her legs accelerated as she ascended a rise.

Someone called her name, but she didn't stop, didn't look back. All her energy focused on getting away from them, running like hell.

A sharp pain stabbed into the center of her back and she fell forward. Her hands scraped on the rocky soil. Struggling, she forced herself to get up and lurched forward.

Her vision blurred. Her knees folded, and she hit the ground. Desperately, she tried to move. It was no use. She'd been shot.

Chapter Twenty-Two

Guns drawn, Shane and the others approached the Stilton house where Carlson was holed up. The deputy who had been watching the house reported that there had been no movement. Carlson hadn't attempted to leave.

At the front door, two men held a battering ram in case they needed to crash through the door. Shane reached out and tried the handle. It was unlocked.

Something was wrong with this setup. Why would Carlson sit here for two hours in the afternoon? He had to be following Neil's orders. Why did Neil want him there?

Shane threw open the door and rushed inside, followed by two other men. They didn't have far to go.

The television set in the front room showed a commercial for shampoo. Carlson was sprawled on the sofa facing the screen. He wasn't moving.

His mouth hung open. His skin was mottled. His sightless eyes bulged in their sockets.

Shane felt at the base of the man's throat for a pulse. Nothing. Standard procedure was to try CPR, but there was no point. "He's dead."

The deputy who had been watching the house spoke up, "I swear nobody got in here. I didn't just sit in my car. I was out, prowling around the house."

On the coffee table in front of the sofa were the contents

of a grease-stained carryout bag: a half-eaten hamburger, fries and a soft drink.

Shane was willing to bet that Carlson had been poisoned by something in the food or drink. Neil and Prentice must have decided that their protégé was a liability. And they had taken him out of the picture.

Deputy Keller—a gray-haired man whose beer belly pushed the limits of his Kevlar vest—took charge. "This here is a crime scene, boys. We need to handle things right. I'll call the sheriff."

Shane stepped back. He should have been glad to see the man who murdered Tom lying dead before him, but this wasn't the way he wanted this situation to play out. With Carlson dead, there was no one to point the finger at Prentice and Neil. And he was damn sure that those two doctors knew how to administer a poison that couldn't be traced back to them. They were about to get away with murder. Again.

His cell phone buzzed. Caller ID showed it was Angela.

She whispered, "Flat tire. Neil grabbed me."

His heart stopped. This was his greatest fear come true. "Where are you?"

"An SUV. In the back." Her voice was barely audible. "Can't talk."

"Angela, are you all right?"

"I was shot."

God, no. He couldn't lose her.

"Can you see through a window. Do you know where you are?"

"Can't tell."

If it was the last thing he ever did, he would get to her in time. Goddammit, he wouldn't let her die. "Leave this phone line open. Give me clues whenever you can."

He clipped his phone onto his ear and strode toward the exit.

"Hey," Keller called after him. "Where the hell do you think you're going?"

"Angela needs me."

ANGELA CURLED INTO A BALL on the floor of Prentice's SUV between the two front seats and the bench seat in the rear. The middle seats were pulled up. It was a strange prison—one that still had a new car smell.

Her only chance to survive this capture was the cell phone. She was lucky that Neil hadn't found it tucked inside her bra. If she could keep feeding information to Shane, he'd find her. Leaving the line open, she returned the phone to her bra.

Though her hands were tied in front of her, she still had a range of motion. Her back ached where she'd been shot. It wasn't as painful as she would have thought. As she became more alert, she seemed to be regaining her strength, rather than fading.

And she didn't see blood.

Twisting around, she dragged herself toward the front of the vehicle.

From the passenger seat, Neil glanced back at her. "You're feeling better already. I knew you would. The dose in the tranquilizer dart was minimal."

"You shot me with a trank gun?" The inside of her mouth tasted as if she'd been chewing on dirty socks. "How could you?"

"It was the best way to control you without hurting you. Why did you take off running?"

"Flat tire. That was how you—" She stopped herself before saying too much. Neil wasn't aware that she knew about Carlson and the black truck parked in Prentice's garage. "That was how Tom died."

"Easy now." He reached between the seats and held a water bottle toward her. "Drink some of this. You'll have a bit of a headache, but otherwise you'll be fine."

When she inched forward to reach the water, she realized that her ankles were bound together. "Untie me. Now."

"The restraints are for your own good. So you won't try something foolish. I don't want to hurt you, Angela."

She took the water bottle from him and drank. He'd been right about the headache, but her mind was clear. The most important thing was to let Shane know where they were.

"Where are you taking me, Neil?"

"I'm going to finish what we started. I'm aware that this isn't the best way to start a marriage, but—"

"I'll never marry you."

From the driver's seat, Prentice gave a short laugh. "You don't have a choice. We already have the marriage license. Obtained by proxy. All we need is a quick blessing, the signature of a minister and it's done."

These two men were crazy, obsessed. And dangerous. She got up on her knees so she could see through the window and look for landmarks. She had to say something to give Shane a clue to their whereabouts. She recognized the road they were on and the body of water beside it. "No wedding. It's not going to happen. I'd rather throw myself out of the car and drown in Beaver Lake."

"Try to be reasonable," Neil said. "We can work things out. For Benjy's sake. The boy needs a father."

"Never mention my son again."

"Oh, please," Prentice said. "You're not a moron, Angela. I'm sure you've figured out by now that I matched your DNA with someone of equal caliber. You must know that Neil is the biological father of your son."

After all their subterfuge, she didn't expect Prentice to be so direct. "I know. I had Benjy's DNA tested."

Neil smiled at her, actually smiled. "So many times, I wanted to tell you. I'm so proud of our son."

Our son? The words sounded obscene when he spoke them. Her anger exploded. "You bastard! You think you're so damn smart. Book smart. But you don't understand a thing about people, about real life. I'll never be your wife. And Benjy will never be your son."

"There's no reasoning with her," Prentice said to Neil. "I told you we'd have to do this the hard way."

Her jaw clenched. "What are you going to do? Kill me?"

"Of course not," Neil said. "But it might be necessary for you to disappear for a while. We have a convenient minister who will sign the certificate with or without you. Ironically, his name is Money. Pastor Money."

"Pastor Money," she repeated, hoping that Shane was listening.

Neil continued, "We'll tell everyone that we went on our honeymoon, and then you'll be hospitalized. It won't be a surprise. Everyone saw how erratic you've been acting, calling off the wedding at the last minute."

And Neil would use a biological claim to solidify his claim for custody. Benjy would fall into his hands. They thought there was nothing she could do to stop them, but she knew better. Carlson would be blamed for Tom's murder, and he would implicate both Prentice and Neil. Ultimately, they'd be in jail, and she'd be free of them.

But she needed to survive long enough for justice to take its course. She decided it was best to let them think she was going along with their insane plan. "It seems as if I don't have a choice."

"Then it's settled," Neil said. "We'll be married."

There was no way of sorting or understanding the avalanche of emotion that crashed over her. Her anger was matched by hopelessness. Her fear overwhelmed by hatred.

More than ever before, she needed Shane's help. One more time, she needed him to ride to her rescue. But she had to give him more to go on.

She played for time. "Can I, at least, clean up before this wedding?"

"I'm sure there's a washroom at the Chapel by the Creek."

"What's that? Chapel by the Creek?"

"Sounds idyllic, doesn't it? That's where we'll be wed." Neil seemed determined to put a good face on the situation. Could he really be so blind? So arrogant that he couldn't for one minute put himself in her shoes? "One day, this will all be a funny story to tell our grandchildren."

She prayed that Shane could hear her, that he would know the location.

CHAPEL BY THE CREEK. Shane knew where it was. And he also knew that Prentice's SUV was approaching on a winding back road that circled Beaver Lake.

He switched on the sirens and the flashing lights atop the official vehicle, and he hit the accelerator. Taking a direct highway route, he could arrive at the chapel before them.

Though backup would be helpful, he couldn't coordinate their arrivals and didn't want to take a chance on spooking Prentice into running.

Plus, he needed to keep listening to Angela's voice on the cell phone. The other voices were muffled and indistinct, but she came through loud and clear. When he'd heard her say that she'd been shot by a trank gun, he felt a sense of relief and he had known, without a doubt, that when this was over he wanted to live every day with her.

Through his phone, he heard her ask how long before they got there. She repeated the answer. "Twenty minutes, more or less."

He flew down the road, careening past the other traffic. He was close to the chapel. It made sense that Prentice would go there. Pastor Money was a nondenominational weirdo who would marry a goat to a chicken if you paid his fee.

He turned off the siren as he neared the chapel, skidded into the parking lot and drove around to the back. Now was the time to call for backup.

WHEN PRENTICE PARKED in front of a white chapel in need of a new paint job, Angela did everything she could to stall. Neil untied the cords around her ankles and helped her to her feet.

She groaned. "I'm a little dizzy. Give me a minute to get my bearings."

"Hurry it up," Prentice snapped. He didn't bother hiding his hostility toward her. "Let's get this over with."

She glared at him. "What's the big rush?"

"I think you know," he said with a sneer. "Carlson called me and told me that someone had broken into my cabin. I'm sure that your boyfriend, Shane, is trying to put together some kind of bogus evidence."

Bogus? Oh, how she wanted to accuse him! She wanted to throw his crimes in his face, but she tried to sound innocent. "I don't know what you're talking about."

"You can't make a case against me without Carlson," he said.

That was true. Their only solid evidence was Carlson's fingerprint at the scene of Tom's murder.

Prentice continued. "Poor Carlson. He has a bad ticker, you know. I wouldn't be surprised if he keeled over from a heart attack at any moment."

"My God, did you kill him, too?"

Neil had finished untying her hands. "Angela, please. I thought you were done with these paranoid delusions."

She stared at him in disbelief. "Are you saying that you don't know about Tom's murder?"

"Your husband was killed in a hit-and-run accident." He took her arm and led her toward the chapel. "I'm beginning to think that you really do need treatment."

She tried to jerk free, and he clamped down more tightly. Prentice held her other arm. Together, they marched her through the door.

The interior of the chapel was as run-down as the outside. The pews were scratched and worn. The carpet runner down the center aisle was a dark, dirty brown. At the front was a simple podium and a table with a white cloth. A man in a long, black robe fussed with a candle arrangement on the table.

"Pastor Money," Neil called to him. "We're here to be married."

Without turning around to face them, he waved them forward. "Yes, yes, get up here."

She dug in her heels, but it was no use. They dragged her down the aisle. She made one last appeal. "You've got to listen to me, Neil. Prentice arranged for Tom's murder. It was Carlson driving the black truck. And now Prentice has probably killed Carlson as well."

Halfway down the aisle, Neil came to a halt. His gaze rested on Prentice, and she saw a flicker of comprehension. "Is she telling the truth?"

"We're scientists, son. There are no facts to back up what she's saying."

Neil dropped her arm and stepped back. "My God, what have you done?"

"I did it for you. And for Benjy."

From outside the chapel, she heard an approaching siren. The man in the black robe whirled around.

It was Shane. His right arm extended straight out from his body. The nose of his gun pointed directly at the center of Prentice's forehead. He growled, "Let her go."

Prentice tried to hide behind her. His hand slipped on her arm, and Angela took advantage of the situation. With all the rage that had been building inside her since they grabbed her, she lashed out. Prentice staggered backward.

She ran toward Shane. In his black robe, he was an impressive figure. He told her to get behind the podium. The approaching sirens got louder.

He stared at Neil. "Are you armed?"

Neil held both hands in the air. "No."

Unwavering, Shane held his aim on Prentice. "You have a gun. Go ahead, make your move."

"If I do, you'll shoot me."

"We call that justifiable homicide," Shane drawled.

Three other lawmen charged through the door at the back of the chapel, and Shane stepped down, willing to leave the arrests to them.

When he turned toward her, she flung her arms around his neck and held on for all she was worth. He was her hero, coming to her rescue again. "I love you, Shane."

He smiled down at her. "It occurs to me that we're standing in a chapel, and Pastor Money is in the back room, ready to perform a wedding."

"Is that a proposition?"

"Marry me, Angela."

Without hesitation, she answered, "I will, but not here. Not today."

"When?"

"Soon enough."

THE NEXT YEAR ON Valentine's Day, Angela stood at the back of a Denver church and waited to marry the man she'd loved as a friend and adored as a lover. Ever since Shane moved into her Denver house, her life had been just about perfect. He loved his work at PRESS. She loved Waffles. In her spare time, she was writing her breakfast recipe cookbook.

Benjy had adapted without a qualm. They were a family, no matter what their DNA makeup.

The trials for Neil and Prentice were still going through appeals, but both men were in jail. Because they'd abducted her, they were denied bail and deemed to be a danger to others.

This would be a small ceremony with only a few good friends and a dinner at Waffles afterward.

She peeked through the open door leading down the aisle and saw Shane standing there in his black suit, looking like the most handsome man on earth. Beside him was his best man, Josh LaMotta, who was still dating Marie, the cake baker.

An infant wailed, and Angela turned toward her half sister, Eve, who had returned to the States with her newborn and her macho military husband.

"Are we ready?" Eve asked.

Benjy stepped up in front of her. "The baby is being loud. We can't start until the baby gets quiet."

Eve leaned down so Benjy was at eye level with the infant. "You tell her."

Benjy kissed the baby on the nose. "Shh."

Miraculously, the child settled down. Eve handed her

daughter off to her husband. She leaned close to Angela and whispered, "Am I noticing a little bulge under that suit?"

"A three-month-old bulge." Angela patted her tummy. "And the best part is that we got pregnant the old-fashioned way."

Yvonne signaled the organist.

Joyfully, Angela went down the aisle.

* * * * *

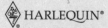 HARLEQUIN®

INTRIGUE

COMING NEXT MONTH

Available October 12, 2010

LARGER-PRINT BOOKS!

GET 2 FREE LARGER-PRINT NOVELS

PLUS 2 FREE GIFTS!

◆ HARLEQUIN®

INTRIGUE®

Breathtaking Romantic Suspense

*See below for a sneak peek at
our inspirational line, Love Inspired®.
Introducing HIS HOLIDAY BRIDE
by bestselling author Jillian Hart*

Autumn Granger gave her horse rein to slide toward the town's new sheriff.

"Hey, there." The man in a brand-new Stetson, black T-shirt, jeans and riding boots held up a hand in greeting. He stepped away from his four-wheel drive with "Sheriff" in black on the doors and waded through the grasses. "I'm new around here."

"I'm Autumn Granger."

"Nice to meet you, Miss Granger. I'm Ford Sherman, from Chicago." He knuckled back his hat, revealing the most handsome face she'd ever seen. Big blue eyes contrasted with his sun-tanned complexion.

"I'm guessing you haven't seen much open land. Out here, you've got to keep an eye on cows or they're going to tear your vehicle apart."

"What?" He whipped around. Sure enough, mammoth black-and-white creatures had started to gnaw on his four-wheel drive. They clustered like a mob, mouths and tongues and teeth bent on destruction. One cow tried to pry the wiper off the windshield, another chewed on the side mirror. Several leaned through the open window, licking the seats.

"Move along, little dogie." He didn't know the first thing about cattle.

The entire herd swiveled their heads to study him curiously. Not a single hoof shifted. The animals soon returned to chewing, licking, digging through his possessions.

Autumn laughed, a warm and wonderful sound. "Thanks,

I needed that." She then pulled a bag from behind her saddle and waved it at the cows. "Look what I have, guys. Cookies."

Cows swung in her direction, and dozens of liquid brown eyes brightened with cookie hopes. As she circled the car, the cattle bounded after her. The earth shook with the force of their powerful hooves.

"Next time, you're on your own, city boy." She tipped her hat. The cowgirl stayed on his mind, the sweetest thing he had ever seen.

Will Ford be able to stick it out in the country
to find out more about Autumn?
Find out in HIS HOLIDAY BRIDE
by bestselling author Jillian Hart,
available in October 2010
only from Love Inspired®.